A
Harlequin
Romance

OTHER

Harlequin Romances

by ESSIE SUMMERS

BEYOND THE FOOTHILLS

by

ESSIE SUMMERS

Harlequin Books

TORONTO • LONDON • NEW YORK • AMSTERDAM • SYDNEY • WINNIPEG

Original hardcover edition published in 1976
by Mills & Boon Limited

ISBN 0-373-02021-X

Harlequin edition published November 1976

Printed in Canada

The author would like to state, for the benefit of the many tourists who visit New Zealand and like to pinpoint localities of books read, that Blue Canyon, for the purpose of this novel, had to be imaginary, but if they visit Lake Wanaka, they can certainly take a tourist bus up the Matukituki Valley and see the backdrop of Mount Aspiring.

CHAPTER ONE

It was glorious fun at the time. They were in high spirits, of course, something engendered by the fact that for ten whole days they'd been free of the classroom, had let their hair down, aired all the problems of teaching, and regained something of the spirit of dedication in which most of them had fared forth from teachers' college a few years ago.

Not that Marilla St. John had ever lost it. Through all the frustrations and exasperations, ninety-five per cent of the time she knew it was the only career for her, satisfying and rewarding.

These courses were so stimulating, so necessary. They were sorry it was at an end. But perhaps it was a pity their male colleagues had just gone off on some ploy of their own when the television interviewer had appeared. He was Marilla's favourite one and he and his team had a sort of roving commission to produce whatever took his fancy. There was a piquancy and variety to his programmes. But variety was just what he wasn't getting now. He'd had it in plenty when he'd asked for views on teaching methods, but when he suddenly asked what their opinions on marriage were, it became very one-sided except for a couple of newly-engaged girls whom the others howled down, saying they were still in love with love. Yes, marriage was getting a poor deal.

Marilla found herself feeling sorry for Benjamin Lemaud, and he was so gorgeous, so light-hearted, with a core of sound philosophy under his debonair manner, probing and revealing the truth in many interviews, in the most acceptable way.

He flung up his hands in mock despair as he reached Marilla, who was sitting on a stone wall, dangling her legs and looking a little rueful because of the way things were going. The camera was off them as he said, 'Now I just

7

hope *you* are going to say something *good* for marriage, something in *praise* of men; this programme isn't going to have any balance, any contrast, any highlights. How about it, love, will you play ball? Besides, in addition to being an interviewer, I'm also a man and a husband to boot, and I'm rapidly developing an inferiority complex. By the time this is finished I'll either crawl away under that clump of primroses, or I'll hie me straight to that professor of psychology who gave you that last lecture, and ask him to sort me out. How *do* you feel on this ... about men and marriage?'

The imp of fun that was never dormant for long at the back of Marilla's mind took over. She was certain that quite a number of the girls didn't really feel so strong on these points, they were simply swayed by the mood of the moment and the present-day trend. Something else stirred in her too, her own recognition of the tremendous way her own mother and father's joy in their marriage had added to their zest in life and the happiness of their home.

Marilla flung her bright hair back, laughed with sheer mischief, looked down on the circle of upturned faces below her and said, 'Here it comes, pals! Suppose you tear me to pieces afterwards, I'm going to be bravely honest and say I think women have a *wonderful* life. It's all theirs ... career first, home-making, the privilege of rearing children, the chance of having a break from earning the daily crust for a few years, the satisfaction of going back to it later if they want to, or being able to keep out of the rat-race and stay home, creating gardens, following their own hobbies and pleasing themselves. The statistics tell us women don't suffer half the coronaries men do in middle age, and in the main, live longer. Perhaps compulsory crust-earning wears them out. But we can please ourselves whether or not we pick up our careers again. If we don't, we can follow all the hobbies we didn't have time for before our marriage ... if that's not freedom, what is?'

'You absolute wizard,' said Benjamin, his whimsical mouth and comical eyebrows curving themselves into laughter lines. 'We'll have that all over again ... in bits and pieces, led by me.' He gave a snap of his fingers to the cameraman.

It would make a wonderful programme ... Marilla with the stiff Wellington wind blowing the red hair back from her shoulders, the vivid green trouser suit, the riot of pink clematis on the wall; behind her the bright gold of a gorse-covered hillside above the high-rise buildings, set against the waters of the exquisitely contoured harbour that was almost cobalt blue today.

Beneath her was the circle of laughing faces and girlish figures in gay attire, some arguing for the sake of arguing, some quite astounded at Marilla because it was the done thing, at the moment, to be on the other side. Some were serious and very sincere about other aspects ... certain injustices that no doubt the female sex did suffer. Marilla herself was only too keen to have those reformed, but to down marriage? *No.*

Benjamin said to her afterwards, over a cup of coffee, 'It was perfect. If you'd been an idealistic youngster of eighteen the viewers would have scoffed that you were a romantic teenager, not yet dry behind the ears, but everything about you, your maturity, your balanced opinions, carried conviction. After all, it wasn't a programme on the rights of women I wanted today, it was a case of what teachers, who handle our children, think of marriage, as a career, as a disaster, as a romantic dream all gossamer and starshine or—' he paused and bit into a cream-filled brandy snap.

'Or a realistic type of happiness, enhancing all the other joys of life and minimising its sorrows and setbacks,' Marilla finished for him.

He nodded, swallowed, said, 'You're just like my wife. She's vital and full of fun and anything but a grizzler. I've never once heard her utter that term: suburban neurosis. She has too many interests, mainly connected with the home and the children. There's never time for all she wants to do, pottery, wood-carving, trying her hand at writing articles, but she revels in family life and puts it first. Oh, she's not a paragon – sometimes, as all mothers do, she finds their pranks a bit much and blows her top, and I try to give her a day off on her own, but I think our children will look back on their childhood as very satisfying. Picnics and bedtime stories and sharing household chores ... and being part of a bigger family circle, with grandparents and aunts and uncles, and their mother sharing their hobbies. We can't tell what's ahead of our children – it's a funny old world – but if they have a happy childhood to remember, they won't grow up with a chip on their shoulder. And as a wife Glenys is so satisfying I sometimes wonder what I did to deserve her.'

Marilla beamed on him. 'I'm so glad about that. We see you so often on TV. You may not even realize how viewers get attached to the different personalities. Equally, one detests some, but all at home like you. You don't put people on the defensive, making them curl up. You bring out the best in them. If, by necessity, it happens to be a critical programme, you hit straight and hard, never below the belt. So I'm glad it was you who did this.' She chuckled, 'It *was* fun, wasn't it?'

He chuckled with her. 'Yes, gave me my light and shade. You were a godsend. I was rapidly getting to the stage of wishing I could have had Glenys on – she was a teacher. But of course that would have been rigging it, or appearing to, even if her ideas are identical with yours. You must meet her. I'll get her to give you a ring and ask you over for a meal.'

As they parted he said, 'Well, if you get a rash of proposals after it, don't forget I'd like to include the wedding in a follow-up programme. You know ... "Sequel to a Benjamin Lemaud Interview." How about that?'

Marilla laughed. 'Sounds a great idea for a comedy. Why don't we sell it to some script-writer? Girl deluged by hundreds of proposals, quite unable to make up her mind.'

He took it up. 'Demented father, at his wits' end, devises great tests of derring-do, based on similar instances in mythology. They line up like gladiators .. how's that?'

Marilla flung out her hands. 'How could I choose? What an intriguing thought! I wonder how a script-writer would handle that? Probably marry me off to some quiet little mouse of a man while the others were fighting it out. Well, it's hardly likely to happen.'

Two weeks later she was wondering how she could have been so naïve, so blind, so carefree. It was no longer a joke ...

Nevertheless, when the programme came on, they all enjoyed it. Marilla's mother had tears in her eyes. 'I think it was very brave of you, Rilla. It's never easy to sound old-fashioned when you're surrounded by people being cynical and worldly-wise. It made that programme. How dull it would have been otherwise. I do appreciate the tribute you gave Angus and myself.'

Helena St. John smiled across the room at her husband. The Reverend Angus St. John grinned back, then looked at his daughter. 'I'd probably never have forgiven you had you made us sound like a couple who'd *never* had a quarrel, but did you have to go to the other extreme? Really, my darling daughter, to say: "Take my parents, for instance – their feeling for each other is so strong that even when they're flaming mad with each other, you still have the feeling they'd rather be having a clanging row with each other than insipidly polite with other people." Marilla, my love, what *do* you think Aunt Myrtle and Dulcie are going to say about *that*?'

Marilla looked horrified. 'I never thought about the aunts! Oh, Dad, heaven help me. They'll quite ignore that I was stressing the fact that you've remained strongly in love with each other and say sarcastically, "You made them sound as if they had a brawl every Saturday night. Really, Marilla, if only you could learn to curb your tongue!" '

'Not to worry, girl ... I've had my aunts too long in my life to care tuppence. I'm used to their grizzling. Their lives are so empty of real things, they need something to complain about. It gives them an interest.' He chuckled. 'I'll never forget their astonishment when they found their pickle of a nephew was going to enter the church. *Their* idea of a minister was someone saintly – preferably with silver hair and a gentle manner. Not a ginger-headed gangly student like me. Even my poor mother was made to believe she'd brought an undesirable element into the family when she produced me. "There has never been a ginger-headed St. John before," Aunt Myrtle said.'

He looked at his daughter more seriously. 'You meant it, didn't you, Rilla, when he asked you what your ideal life would be? When you said: "Some high-country sheep station beyond the foothills, living in some old homestead, rich with history." I thought I detected a note of real nostalgia. You've never got over missing Fairlie, have you?'

Marilla said swiftly, 'Oh, Dad, when your father's a minister and you move on from parish to parish, there are compensations. It's good for you. You learn to take change in your stride. I don't regret any of our moves, really. But now you've got your Moderatorial Year over, I think I might take off for a South Island township against the mountains if I can get a teaching position in the vicinity. As a matter of fact I've been scanning the Gazettes for one lately, but there's been none I really fancied. Though this is the time – from now on – when they'll appear. Now Kit and Fiona are older I thought you mightn't miss me so much. And it looks as if Guy will be back here next year.'

Her mother's reaction was swift. 'I wish you would. We've had you home longer than some parents do, and I'll never forget that as soon as you knew your father was to be made Moderator you decided to stay home so I could travel round the parishes with him. I couldn't have gone with an easy mind otherwise – not with Granny so frail. But you're free now. You've had this course, to pep you up. There'll be plenty of relieving teaching posts here for you till the end of the year, to give you time to pick and choose a situation that will really suit you.'

The Reverend Angus looked rueful. 'We'll miss you like nobody's business, but it's time you got out on your own, Marilla. If you stay here in the parish you'll get more and more piled on you.'

Marilla grinned. 'I rather feel you've been discussing this. Are you afraid I'll remain a spinster all the days of my life?'

Angus snorted. 'What nonsense – and you know it's nonsense. Like Benjamin Lemaud said, "How come a girl like you with ideas like yours hasn't married long since?" You've never really fallen in love, have you, Rilla? It was true what you answered him ... that you were still waiting for the right man to come along and that you'd never settle for second-best.'

Marilla looked serious. 'I've had moments of thinking I was on the verge of falling in love, and I'm not stupid enough to feel he must be ideal in every way, but I've never met anyone I'd really want to spend the rest of my life with. I've enjoyed them as dance partners, to go skiing with on Ruapehu, or water-skiing or boating with, but no, I want someone like you, Dad.'

Her father put his head back and roared. 'That settles it! If you're going to get a father fixation, I'm going to expel you from the nest. Try for a school in South Canterbury or further down, against the lakes.' He looked mock-serious. 'But you never know – some high-country station-owner might easily decide, after that programme, that you're his ideal woman and propose. Some poor guy who hitherto has fallen for girls who prefer the city and who suddenly realizes here's one made to order.'

'You mad thing, Dad! Most high-country men marry high-country wives, daughters of their neighbours. Oh dear, there's the phone. I knew it! Every jolly parishioner will ring up to say they've seen it, and talk for ages. Dad, you answer it. Don't let on I'm home.'

Angus St. John went to the phone on the living-room desk, said, after a moment or two, 'Yes, she's available, I'll call her.' He put his hand over the mouthpiece, said, a line between his brows, 'Do you know anyone in South Westland, Marilla? It's a person-to-person call. A Callum McMullison.'

'Callum McMullison? What a gorgeous name. But no, I don't know him – it must be a mistake. Don't let them connect us. Ask the exchange are they sure he wants me?'

Angus spoke again, then said, 'Yes, it's you all right.'

Marilla knew a curious reluctance to take the phone. She was a little reassured when the voice sounded like an older man's. He came to the point extremely quickly. He'd just seen the programme on the Network, and would like to fly to Wellington next week to meet her. He'd had the pleasure of hearing her father at Greymouth on his Moderatorial tour. Would she be home?

Her parents saw Marilla's eyes go glassy. She uttered a sound that was little more than a bleat. Then she pulled herself together and said in what she hoped was a firm, schoolmarmish tone, 'What on earth would you want to do that for? You're a perfect stranger to me. I'm afraid—'

Then as he interrupted and she listened, she swallowed. She turned and looked at her father and mother with startled eyes. They caught on and looked almost equally startled. Then Marilla said slowly and distinctly, 'I think you must be clean mad.' She was tempted to put the receiver up, but couldn't quite bring herself to do it. She said coldly, 'I was roped into the programme on the spur of the moment. I can assure you I wasn't thinking of it as a sort of modern matrimonial advertising medium. I hope it doesn't take anyone else this way. No, you may *not* fly up to see me. Now don't, please. *Goodbye!*'

She hung up, and sat down, her knees oddly weak. 'This is ghastly! I – I could have every lonely nut in the high-country thinking I'd make a mountain man an ideal wife! Oh, no, that's stupid. I mustn't panic. I mean, surely not more than one crank would act on impulse like that. He's bought a run down near the glaciers. Cattle, not sheep, he said apologetically. As if it mattered to me! When I asked why he wanted to see me, he said promptly and unashamedly, "View matrimony, of course," and proceeded to tell me he'd built a small new home on the property but there was an old homestead on it he'd only be too pleased to restore and we could let a married couple have the new place. *We.* As if it was all settled! He's nuts. Oh, dear—' she sprang up as the phone rang right by her side. 'Dad, if it's anyone I don't know, I'm not speaking to them.'

It was just the first of half a dozen calls from friends and parishioners who'd thoroughly enjoyed the programme. Marilla began to relax. She began answering herself to save her father, who surely deserved an uninterrupted hour or so with his book on this rare night home. But she chilled when another personal call was announced from the far North. However, it said Jocelyn Merridew calling Miss Marilla St. John. Oh, fine. Just some woman who shared her views, perhaps.

A charming but unmistakably masculine voice greeted her. Marilla said quickly, 'I thought the exchange said a woman.'

There was an equally charming chuckle. 'It's this name of mine . . . like Beverley, and Carol, it can be used for either sex. Don't let it put you off.' His approach was rather more oblique. At first, that was. He said how much he'd enjoyed the programme; how refreshing it was to get a viewpoint like that. He chatted on, with Marilla trying to be as non-committal as possible, and then cutting in and saying, 'Well, it was very kind of you to ring, Mr. Merridew, and thank you very much, but I rather think my father wants to use the phone, would you—'

The voice said, 'Don't go yet, please.' He said he and his sister would like to invite her to visit them. Sorry it wasn't a sheep station, which she obviously preferred. They ran cattle. Their land went right down to the sea. Glorious bathing, marvellous spot for a holiday. You couldn't see another house far as the eye could roam. They had an old style Colonial house. They had a tennis-court, their own nine-hole golf-course. The weather was marvellous right now, and she'd said she wasn't in a permanent teaching position, so how about it?

It sounded magnificent – if only it had been an offer coming from friends – not because of that programme. It was obvious what lay behind the offer. She said firmly that relieving teachers were in such demand she wasn't free just now. It was very good of himself and his sister, but it wouldn't be possible later as she was already booked for a Southern holiday when the year ended. She added, 'I'm sure you and your sister have a lovely home and it was generous of you to offer this to a total stranger.'

His voice warmed, 'Oh, but I don't feel you are a stranger. I feel you're a kindred spirit. I think you'd love it here.'

Marilla's voice crisped, with a note of finality. 'I'm very appreciative, of course, but no. Besides, your sister mightn't really relish having a stranger wished on her – thank you, but I—'

'My sister is as keen as I am. It was she who yanked me out of my farm office to watch the programme, as soon as you came on.' He hesitated. 'I – I ought to tell you that she's just housekeeping for me till she marries a farmer neighbour early next year. Our parents have just retired to Kaitaia. I—'

That finished Marilla. They'd hatched this plot together. She said abruptly, 'I'm afraid I must go. I can hear a visitor coming. Glad you enjoyed the programme ... goodbye.' And before he could think of something else, she put the receiver down.

Certainly someone was coming in – Kit, followed by Fiona, who looked amazed to find their father and mother helpless with laughter, rolling about the couch. The twins were just back from some Varsity function. 'How was the programme?' they asked in duet. 'If only we hadn't missed it. We heard on the way home it was absolutely smashing.'

'That's a fair description,' said Marilla, sinking back weakly. 'In fact, devastating. It's going to ruin the peace of our home if this goes on. But it can't, surely.'

But it could and did. It stopped being the huge joke Kit and Fiona thought it. Marilla became the butt of jokes at home and abroad. Her father thought it amusing the next Sunday when he had more strange young men in his congregation than ever before. Even her mother didn't take it as seriously as Marilla. 'I know it's annoying, Rilla, but on the other hand it must be doing a lot for your ego. I mean, let's face it, we women may ignore wolf-whistles, but it does a lot for one's morale, after all. Don't lose your sense of humour over it, will you?' She giggled, 'Whatever would your father's aunts say if they heard me talking of enjoying wolf-whistles?'

Marilla hugged her. 'With a figure like yours, pet, no wonder you get them still?'

'Only from the rear.' Helena St. John sounded mock-regretful. 'If I turn round and they see my lined visage, they get such a shock, poor dears.'

'You utter idiot! You sound as if you think your face is wrinkled like a crab-apple. You still have a bloom.'

'A rapidly fading bloom. Oh, I meant to tell you. After Myrtle rang up to express their disapproval of you having said that about us sometimes being flaming mad with each other, Elfreda slipped out to a phone-box and rang to say *she* had thought the whole thing perfectly splendid, no humbug, and really exciting, and not to let you be hurt by anything Myrtle or Dulcie might say. Poor wee Elfreda! How different life would save been had her parents lived, or her guardians been of this day and age. She was too gentle. They were too domineering. They talked duty, duty, duty to her, till she hadn't a mind of her own left.

'Well, Rilla, you've got the worst over. These things are nine days' wonders, no more. There's a limit to how many high-country farmers want a wife.'

Marilla pulled a face. 'Trouble is, Mother, it didn't stop at the farmers. There were all those others who thought here was a girl who obviously wanted marriage and was flaunting her sweetness unseen upon the desert air ... they were sure I'd fall in love with them and settle for marriage in suburbia.'

Helena looked at her daughter with shrewd eyes.

'They've got something there. If you fall in love, Marilla, you'll take whatever life the man offers, ideal for your temperament or not. I had two school friends. Evelyn wanted a city life, security, golf, musical functions, and a beautiful garden. She married an engineer with the Ministry of Works, forever pushing roads through hitherto inaccessible places, bridging rivers and tunnelling through mountains, yet now she pities the stay-at-home wives. Jean wanted to marry an explorer or a mountaineer, and seems very contented as the wife of a stockbroker. They simply followed their men.'

'Fine,' said Marilla sourly, 'but *they* didn't publicly advertise their preferences like I did, fool that I was. I can see months ahead of me trying to convince vain young men that though I may have said I was still waiting for Mr. Right to appear, I'm not exactly desperate for a husband. As for using public transport – like yesterday, when I was having the battery recharged – no fewer than three young men spoke to me, to ask wasn't I the girl on that programme? I could see it dawning in their eyes. Two on the train, one on the bus. I pretended complete ignorance – hadn't seen the programme, didn't know what they were talking about.'

She grew over-sensitive about the staff-room jokes as time went by, of the letters from remote places that reached her asking for a closer acquaintance, for a pen-friendship. She felt churlish as she answered them curtly, but if she didn't answer, they rang to find out hadn't she got the letters. She felt her temper cracking under the strain. A few artless – or not so artless – remarks from pupils got under her skin.

Twice a man Marilla distrusted on sight turned up to wait for her outside one of the city schools. The Headmaster was sharp with her. 'You must get rid of him immediately and finally, or I'll have to stop having you, efficient and all as you are. I can't have undesirables hanging round, parents will start complaining.'

Marilla had to take her courage in both hands, walk up to the man, and tell him she wouldn't be coming back to this school, and that if he was seen there again, the Head would put the police on to him.

It didn't matter much because one of the Bay schools, her own favourite, was only too pleased to have her for longer periods. The man from South Westland and the one from the far North both followed up their phone calls, which they repeated, by flying to Wellington and coming to the house. Jocelyn Merridew was favoured by Helena. He was extremely attractive. Helena said to her daughter, 'I think you ought to give yourself the chance to get to know him – you make up your mind far too quickly about men, Marilla, not just now, but you always have.'

Marilla sighed. 'My dear mama, I know Jocelyn is a very nice chap, but there's not a spark of feeling – in that way – for him within me.' Helena gave up and very regretfully watched him go.

Callum McMullison was a horse of another colour, very persistent. Marilla actually felt a revulsion towards him. He stayed in the Capital a week. Finally Marilla sent him away with a flea in his ear. She couldn't help it.

Helena was dusting the lounge windowsill as he went down the path. He bent down, picked up a bamboo stake she'd had left over from staking the young delphiniums earlier, and took a vicious swipe at the row of ranunculi that were the pride of her heart and then he slammed the garden gate with a crash all the neighbours would hear.

She went out to Marilla, who had angry patches of red in rather white cheeks. She tried to make a joke of it. 'My garden will look as if it's been visited by a tornado shortly, if we get many more like him. I take it he's gone for good?'

Marilla said miserably, 'I did what I vowed I wouldn't . . . lost my temper with him. The things he said! Said he reckoned the interview couldn't have been on the level – that it was just a gimmick I'd been put up to – that I was no more like that girl on TV than a machine. That I was completely cold, that I must have learned it all off by rote! Boy, I got into red-hot fury then – he even backed off. Must have had his mind changed for him about *that*.

'Then he turned really nasty, said in that case, was I keeping tally of everyone's resources and would I close with the most advantageous offer? Oh, Mum, I feel so humiliated! I actually stamped my foot and yelled at him. And he slammed the door so hard, Granny's violet jar fell off the mantelpiece and smashed on the hearth – look—' she held it out, in fragments.

Her mother took it calmly. 'It will mend. It may never hold water again, but it can go in the cabinet with our other keepsakes. My mother never fashed herself over breakages. She said people were more important, and nobody purposely breaks things, even children. I'm only sorry you were home this morning. I'd made up my mind if he came again I was going to send him packing. As soon as you've had a snack and some coffee, you'd better get out to the Bay School. That'll take your mind off things.'

It hadn't. It was such a shock when the Head sent for her after school and she went expecting instructions and received what amounted to a proposal instead. She thought the world of him, and he desperately needed a wife, and a mother for his two children. He'd had a succession of indifferent housekeepers since his wife had died.

If she'd had one spark of feeling for him, she'd have considered it. He said wistfully, 'I know I'm rather old for you, but I've been so attracted and didn't dare chance my luck till now. That programme revealed you as all I'd hoped you might be, and so mature that I thought it might cancel out some of the years.'

Marilla knew she mustn't raise any hopes, that it would be cruel to be kind, to let him take her out. She managed to turn him down without inflicting too deep a hurt, she thought. She told him she was immensely flattered by this, but in actual fact she had had such a skinful of the publicity, she was going down South away from it all.

It was the last straw, on reaching home, to find the aunts'

car parked in the drive. Dad wouldn't be home, either, to deflect their aim. They would get at Mother through Marilla. They hadn't wanted their nephew to marry Helena Stewart, a young war widow with a small son. They'd had him marked down for a friend's daughter, a tall, elegant creature with as much personality, Father had told them, as a bowl of blancmange.

Mother had laughed. 'And what dish did I remind you of, Angus?'

He'd grinned. 'An Indian curry, stimulating to the palate, but hot as hell and occasionally bad for the digestion. My favourite!'

The aunts must have been mad. Dad had been fresh from a prisoner-of-war camp after being rescued from the Mediterranean when his ship went down. He hadn't wanted simpering elegance – he'd wanted Helena's maturity, the way she was facing life, as gaily as she could, because children ought to be brought up surrounded by happiness, not grief.

But now the Aunts were here. Marilla felt like fleeing. But she'd have to face them some time. They hadn't come near since the programme. She'd hoped they were too disgusted.

Poor Cousin Elfreda would sit there looking distressed. Why hadn't she broken away long ago? The children's books she wrote so well had made her independent financially. She would be wearing something pastel and ladylike, almost melting into her background, mouse-like and self-effacing, apart from now and then giving Marilla timidly sympathetic glances. If by ill-luck Aunt Myrtle intercepted one, she would quell her by saying: 'Yes, Elfie, *did* you want to say something?' in a tone that hardly supposed her opinions could matter in the slightest. Father's Aunts were absolute anachronisms.

So Marilla got a terrific shock when she entered to find Elfreda in a bright tangerine trouser suit that set off her willowy figure to perfection, and focused eyes upon her. What was more, she was perched on the table swinging her legs and she had the most ridiculous shoes on. Flamboyant shoes, they were, with multi-striped insets. She was jangling some curious ultra-modern bracelets on her slim wrists and — yes, it was true — she had bright chestnut glints in her hair. What an improvement!

As Marilla came in Elfreda said, 'Oh, hullo, Marilla. I've been dying to see you. What a marvellous time you've been having. Is there going to be a follow-up programme?'

'God forbid!' ejaculated Aunt Myrtle. 'Elfie, will you please behave and stop trying to encourage her! I was afraid of this.'

Elfreda looked across at her and grinned in a sort of gamin way. 'Watch it, Aunt. I've told you I won't answer to that ridiculous name any more. It may have been all right at six, but not at forty-two. Marilla, they've come over to berate you, but I'm here to see they don't. You should be enjoying every moment of this. *I* would!'

Marilla boggled, then, recovering, said, 'Elfreda, it's been horrible. I'm frightened to answer the phone or the door. I hate opening mail. Some of them are so peculiar.'

Aunt Myrtle looked triumphant. 'See, Elfreda? Even Marilla thinks she's overstepped the bounds of common sense this time. My great-niece has made not only herself a laughing stock, but us!'

Marilla was staring at Elfreda. Funny she'd never noticed what an urchin type of face she had. Now her eyes crinkled up and disappeared into slits of mirth. 'Oh, what's a few phone calls? If I were Marilla I'd visit them all in turn and decide which one I loved the best. Most girls would envy you the chance ... able to pick and choose. I could go along with you, Marilla, as chaperon. I'd love it, visiting all those farms. After all, if I'd been able to marry the man I wanted to, you'd have spent all your holidays with me in the high country and ten to one you'd have married in the same district.'

Aunt Myrtle's voice sounded almost agonized. 'Elfreda!' But at least she'd dropped the 'Elfie.'

It was the first hint of romance in Elfreda's life Marilla had heard of. But she turned and said, 'Aunt Myrtle, how

22

has it made *you* a laughing stock?'

'It was a topic of conversation at the Club.'

'The interview? Well, wouldn't those respectable matrons applaud a girl who approved of marriage?' Oddly enough this was making Marilla feel less serious about it.

'Not so much the interview – the consequences. It's got out – I believe Elfreda is responsible – that you're having proposals from the length and breadth of New Zealand. You've made an exhibition of yourself and made us all look foolish.'

Marilla considered this. 'Not *entirely* the length and breadth, Aunt. There's not been one from Stewart Island. Just imagine – some poor lonely fisherman on Thule or somewhere doesn't have power or TV – if only he knew what he'd missed! And there weren't any from Cape Reinga . . . but then there aren't any mountains there, just a lighthouse – so perhaps it's just as well. Come to think of it, I haven't had any offers from the Chatham Islands either.'

Dulcie came in, 'Marilla, *you* may think it no end of a lark, *we* certainly don't. You know Myrtle is in the directory as Miss M. St. John. We've been pestered with calls.'

Elfreda dimpled. 'If only they weren't quite so young! I'd have suggested they called on us instead. *Three* unclaimed treasures, no less. They could have had their pick!'

Aunt Myrtle's voice had lost its militant stridency. It was reduced to a bleat. 'Elfreda!'

Marilla said, 'I did have one about your age, Elfreda, from South Westland. He phoned, he wrote, he flew up to see me. What a pity he and I had such a violent row this morning. He smashed Gran's vase as he went, then took all the tops of Mother's ranunculi as he went out of the gate. So on second thoughts, I don't think he'd do you. I feel a real gentleman would have taken his – his – what's the word I want?'

Elfreda said solemnly, 'Congé, that's it. He'd have taken his congé in a more seemly fashion. Isn't it a

23

gorgeous word? It makes me think of knee-breeches, and asking papa for his daughter's hand. But it's all very interesting, isn't it, Rilla?

'No one will ever be able to twit *you* with being on the shelf, will they? Though that's one thing about the present day, they don't.'

Suddenly Marilla's mother succumbed to the giggles. Myrtle and Dulcie regarded her with disgust. The next moment Elfreda and Marilla joined in.

Marilla sobered up, snatched at her handkerchief, mopped her eyes. 'Oh, Elfreda, you've done me good. I was making myself miserable over the whole thing. Perhaps I got it out of perspective. I was on the point of taking myself off down South. In fact, I will go. I've got no relieving booked in for next week, except I could go to the Bay, if I wanted to, but – but I'd rather not, anyway.

'I'll give myself a holiday. You can send the Gazettes down after me, Mother, and I'll pick out a South Island job from one. But don't tell anyone where I am. I'll get a job to start in February, and meanwhile I'll just enjoy myself. By that time, the would-be suitors will have found more willing brides. Aunt Myrtle, I'm sorry you got drawn into this, but I couldn't have foreseen it. It's a pity that our name is an unusual one – Smith would have discouraged them.

'I'll get away on Saturday. If any letters come from strangers, return them to senders. If I get sick of holidaying, I could take relieving down South.'

Elfreda swung off the table. 'I've got a notion about that. Come along to Angus's study. You may not like the idea and I don't want anyone to persuade you into it, or out of it.' She glanced significantly at the Aunts, so Marilla's mother said hurriedly, 'I'll make us a cup of tea while you discuss it.'

With the study door safely shut, Marilla said to Elfreda, laughter brimming over, 'Good for you. What's come over you?'

Elfreda shrugged. 'I won't go into that in detail – take too long. I've just stopped being a coward, that's all. I've been spineless all these years. But not any more – I've got back my self-respect and confidence. I'll just say that long ago I thought the man I loved hadn't loved me enough to try to patch up the quarrel we had. Just lately I found out he had. But Aunt Myrtle saw to it that he didn't see me. It doesn't matter any longer, of course – but it did something to me. What matters is you.

'I ran into an old friend yesterday. The daughter of a friend of hers is married to a sheep farmer in a remote valley away in from Lake Wanaka in Central Otago. She's been teaching her children by correspondence lessons but wants a governess for them next year as she's going to try for another baby. Oh dear, Aunt Myrtle would think that was a coarse way of putting it. She lost a baby before birth about three years ago through over-doing it at shearing-time, and they feel if someone could take over the oversight of the lessons and keep an eye on the children out of school hours, it would help tremendously.

'It's your kind of country, Marilla. You like riding, and they're opening up a new ski-field above there. Access may go through their valley. In any case, they sometimes even use skis to go round the sheep. They must have someone who can take that sort of life. I said at the time it sounded exactly the sort of job my cousin's girl would be interested in.'

'Elfreda, I'd love it, if they'd have me. But I don't think I could face it if they knew who I was, and my views on the ideal married life. I mean, wanting a high-country setting. They'd think I was after any bachelor neighbours there might be up there. Marilla St. John is so unusual a name. They'd click.'

Elfreda said calmly, 'There aren't any neighbours. The whole valley is theirs. I very much doubt if they have television. Some of the back-country runs have them, but mostly when several farmers can club together for the cost of a translator. Anyway, why not apply under your first name? Eleanor St. John. Marilla, I realize, might ring a bell if they have by any chance seen it.'

Marilla considered it. 'All right, I'll do just that. Give me the address and I'll get it away tonight. You'd better give me the name of your friend.'

'Write Mrs. Donal MacGillivray, Blue Canyon Station, Waihemo Valley, Private Bag, Wanaka. They just pick up their mail when they go in. It'll take time to get a reply, but if you want to go South now, your mother will know where to forward a reply. You could even go in to see them if it's favourable – and I'm sure it would be, with your qualifications and Mrs. Granville's personal recommendation of you as my cousin. I expect they won't want you till February for the new school year, but if you're away for a bit, this hoo-ha will have died down and you could come home for Christmas.'

'Elfreda, this is marvellous. Do you know this place? I can vaguely remember when we lived at Fairlie, you having a holiday at Lake Wanaka. You saw us on the way back to Wellington.'

'Yes. I was staying with Brigid Granville when I first saw Blue Canyon. It's glorious. You go in off the Matukituki Valley – this valley wasn't as open or sunlit till you got right in through the Gorge. The Blue River is so deep that even in the gorge there's no rough white water tumbling through, it's deep blue – hence the name. It's remote and incredibly beautiful ... a sort of Ultima Thule.'

'It sounds like heaven,' said Marilla. 'And praise the saints this Donal MacGillivray is a much married man. No bachelor station-owners for me. I hope their station-hands are all married too. Elfreda, if I get the position, might it be possible for you to come South and come to Blue Canyon for a holiday? Sheep stations are known for hospitality. Wouldn't you like to recapture a little of the enchantment it evidently had for you once?'

Elfreda laughed but shook her head. 'Would you understand if I said I wouldn't want to go back? It can be a mistake. Remember Bruce More? He went back to Britain for a trip, and wanted to revisit the village in Cumberland where he'd had a memorable boyhood holiday. He found it all right, but the cottage where he had stayed had been bulldozed down to make way for a new housing estate, even the wall he'd climbed, with its roses and sweet peas, to watch the iron-ore miners, red with dust, alighting from their train every night, was only a scar on the ground, and the village green had completely disappeared. No, Marilla. I'll just remember Blue Canyon as it was.'

CHAPTER TWO

MARILLA ought to have been surfeited with beauty by the time she reached Lake Wanaka, after the hundreds of miles, by ship through the Queen Charlotte Sounds, then through the tobacco-fields, hop-fields and apple-lands of Nelson and right down the narrow strip of Westland, bordered on one side by the remote headlands and dashing spray of the Tasman Sea and the other by the Alps in all their glory of glaciers and rain forest; nevertheless, after driving through the savage and awesome grandeur of the Haast Pass, she thought this dreaming township set in a semi-circle round the blue waters, and splashed vividly with the rainbow hues of a myriad wild lupins, of golden broom and tangerine Californian poppies, was the loveliest yet.

Till now, mindful of the fact this could be an extended holiday, she'd stayed at camps, but the shaven perfection of the lawns and alpine gardens round the Wanaka Hotel and its air of modern luxury tempted her. Prince Charles had stayed here ... why not live like royalty for one night?

The next morning the weather forecast was so good, Marilla decided to waste no time in inspecting the Wai-hemo Valley. It was a scenic road, she was told, open to tourists, so the family wouldn't suspect she was looking over the territory. She would be just one more car coming and going, this blue and golden day.

She drove along the shoreline, turning sharply right where stands of huge chestnuts, limes and oaks almost met overhead. To her left the Hawthenden Motels sat on the hill in glorious farmland. She'd more than likely book in there tonight.

This road to Glendhu Bay was superb, even tar-sealed. It was just over thirty-five miles to Blue Canyon. On her right the vast lake disappeared into the stretched-out arms of great mountains, and Ruby Island, tree-studded and shaped like an oval salver, seemed to float just off-shore. There was such symmetry about this lake, cast in a more gentle mould than some of the other lakes which were angled and dramatic.

The first splendid view of Mount Aspiring came into view across that cornflower blue and she pulled in to photograph it for Elfreda, who had said, with almost a catch in her voice, 'It may be about two and a half thousand feet less than Mount Cook, but Mount Aspiring's sculpted ridges and pyramidal cone have a sort of eth-ereal beauty that, to me, far surpasses it.'

Marilla, as befitting one born and bred in the shadow of Cook, had doubted that. Aorangi, the Cloud-piercer, as their father had preferred to call it, had been part of his parish. But now she understood. There was a fæery-like quality about this, remote and delicate, a mountain of dreams. No wonder they called it the Matterhorn of New Zealand! Elfreda had said the roar of its avalanches could be heard in Wanaka itself.

She wondered how long Elfreda's holiday had lasted. She'd mentioned that she might have married a high-country man. Perhaps she had met him somewhere here.

This road was sheer enchantment, immaculate home-steads in jewels of settings, range upon range of foothills melting into the alpine peaks. The road dipped, climbed, crossed a small river, the Motatapu, then the landscape widened out into the sunlit Matukituki Valley where on the river-flats below waterfall-laced heights, bronze-flanked Herefords and snow-fleeced Romneys grazed.

On her right the river swept fiercely against the bluffs on the far side on its way to the lake she could no longer see. How aptly named, the dashing or pounding stream, ice-cold with snow-water, even on a cloudless day like this. Just as well it was, in this heavy rainfall area. She'd been warned that when she turned off near the Phoebe Burn, the fords would start – shallow now, but in a sudden downpour their rise could be remarkable.

She turned in under Black Peak, layered with thousands of feet of schist, upthrust by who knew what ancient upheavals. The fords began. Marilla took them slowly, careful not to create too much splashing, and avoiding the larger boulders brought down by rains. She followed her father's instructions, using her brakes to dry them out after each one.

The signpost had said: 'Blue Canyon 12 miles. No exit. Proceed with extreme care.' She crossed a small one-way bridge and entered the Canyon. Here was a different world, shadowed and narrow. After the first bend the road overhung a river so far below one felt suspended. Not that it climbed much, it was merely that through countless ages this snow-fed river, unable to wear away to any extent the narrow iron-clad heights, had deepened its bed to a frightening extent.

Elfreda had told her there was no bridge over the Blue River in the Canyon, because the road kept to the eastern side and the river wound back on its tracks, going west before finding a way out to join the Matukituki. So at least the homestead was never cut off by flood, only by snow.

Sometimes the bluffs, glinting with mica, overhung the road, cutting out any sun. It was very narrow, with infrequent passing-places. Marilla hoped she'd meet no huge sheep-trucks bringing stock out. Because if so, she'd be the one to do the backing to a passing-place. The one on the outside edge never did it.

Goodness, still five miles to go. On her left a hanging valley spilled a waterfall in three gigantic leaps. What volume! Of course, the map had said Leap-frog Falls. Then she was near the homestead. Where did all that water go? There must be another river against those bluffs. Of course, it would be the Waihemo. Didn't that mean something like the Disappearing Water? It certainly couldn't be seen from here.

What a road! Grass grew between the ruts, stones flew up and bashed against the undercarriage; she hoped no damage would result. And the fords were countless. She saw sheep-pens, cattle-yards, a hay-barn, went through some poplars, and there it lay, the homestead, just as El-freda had described it, cream-washed stone, with lattices for roses and creepers against it, its shutters a warm brown, its steeply gabled roof green, a four-square sturdy house, as if there for ever, defying these mountain climes, the fierce blistering sun, the battling, pitiless winds, the intense frosts.

Across from the old homestead, on the hill to the left, was the modern ranch-style home that the Donal Mac-Gillivrays were building to move into, Elfreda's friend had told her. It was delightful too, incorporating the motif of its surroundings in a jigsaw of stones from the mountains set into its walls to give its corners strength, but interspersed with cedar-wood oiled to a colour just a little darker than the flanks of those grazing Herefords. A house that would be easier to run, and built to the sun, yet ... her eyes turned to the other. Here was a house that looked as if it sat with its hands folded in its lap waiting for someone to come along and demand a story from it.

Marilla knew, instantly, that if her mother sent down a letter saying she'd got the position, she would have no hesitation in coming here, despite its loneliness. Not a sign of life was visible. She would go on to that far terrace, pull off the road, have a cup of coffee from her flask. If anyone came out she might make herself known, inquire if she had been accepted. Or might it seem too eager? Her indecision tempted her to postponement. She'd explore beyond the next ford on foot. Certainly she wouldn't take the car through that one. It was fit only for Rovers or jeeps. She opened the boot and drew out the calf-high gumboots Mother had fussily insisted on stowing there, with winter-weight sweaters and a bottle of cough-mixture!

The chill of the water struck right through the rubber. On the far side, plodding on, she found the road stretched up round a bluff with a blind corner that drew her like a magnet. What view might it conceal? Corner after corner lured her on. Never had she seen any place that captivated her more. Oh, she must, must get that position.

These were the rough private roads that stretched right into the interior. Access roads for trampers.

Suddenly, to her alarm, she realized the sun was westering and among those heights it could dip with black-out suddenness. She must hurry back to the car. That Gorge Road would be steeped in inky darkness after sunset. So she wouldn't call at the homestead today. To her great surprise, she had noticed telephone wires. In Elfreda's day they'd just had a two-way radio. So she'd hasten back to the motels, and ring the homestead from there tonight, asking if she might come out for a personal interview the next day.

She flung her wet boots into the boot of the car, after the return journey taking her longer than she'd liked, pressed the self-starter. Nothing happened. Oh well, not to panic, the engine would be cold. The battery had just been recharged, so it would start in a moment. Perhaps she had flooded it with the choke.

Twenty sweating minutes later she knew she would have to ask for help. Pity she'd parked the car so far past. That drive was a long one, too. What if no one was home? But surely there would be house cows to milk? How ghastly if they didn't come home till after dark!

As she neared her heart lightened. She saw a thin blue spiral of smoke from a chimney. Now what should she do? Make herself known from the start, or merely let them think she was a tourist whose car had conked out? Perhaps it was a loose wire. Men could usually fix these things in a jiffy. It would take time to explain who she was – and that sun was rapidly setting. And what an introduction! They'd think her a helpless dill not at all suited to the life here. Well, she'd play it by ear. See what they were like.

She was just raising her hand to the knocker when the door was yanked open so forcibly she almost fell in, feeling extremely stupid as she teetered, and made a wild clutch at the jamb.

A tall, broad figure loomed above her. It had red hair even more aggressively bright than her own, and fierce

32

eyebrows. Donal MacGillivray, she presumed. Before she could get a word out he barked: 'Are you the owner of that little Mini down there?'

She repressed a desire to retort childishly: 'Most Minis *are* little,' but got no further than a nod before he said, 'How long have you been there? I've just seen you. It'll take you busy to get through the Gorge before dark – have you any idea what that road's like in darkness? Or are you only used to lighted city streets?'

It got her back up. 'No, I'm not. I was born and brought up not far from Mount Cook!'

'Well, I shouldn't say it's taught you much. You must get going and waste no time.'

She swallowed. 'That's just what I can't do – get going. For some inexplicable reason I can't get a spark out of her. My tank has plenty of petrol, my battery's newly charged, but—'

'But you had no idea that fording streams in a car that size plays merry hell with it. Sprays water all up round the engine and gets into the distributor and you've no show of starting her till it's dried out. I don't suppose you thought of trying to do it with a duster? And it would be too much to expect you to carry a can of C.R.C., I imagine? A drying spray. No one ought to go into country like this without. You might have been held up in the Canyon, a menace to yourself and all other traffic. Or stranded there all night, alone. You're damned lucky it happened here.'

Marilla felt her hackles rise. 'That's what *I* thought . . . *at first!* But I appear to have roused a sleeping ogre. All my experience has led me to believe high-country folk are noted for hospitality – and resource. I'll try drying it out with a duster. Or if you've got one of those thingamyjigs you mentioned, I'll borrow it and see what I can do.'

'And could you recognize a distributor if you saw one?'

She bit her lip. 'No, but I'm sure you'd love to describe one to me, and I'll do my fool best.' She found herself glaring at him. Oh dear, two redheads in this situation was just awful. All her high-falutin' notions about this place being a veritable Eden were disappearing. No wonder Mrs. Donal found it hard to get governesses. He'd expect them to be able to cope with any situation, plus teaching his probably redheaded, bad-tempered brats everything from ABC to higher mathematics. Just let him wait! She'd write from Wanaka saying she'd called to look the place over but had met such utter rudeness, she thought she could do better elsewhere, with a homestead of more civilized people! And she hoped Mrs. Donal would chew his ear. Even thinking of writing the letter relieved her feelings . . . if she ever did.

What was he saying? 'Your fool best would probably describe it to perfection. I'll get my spray and come.'

'Thank you,' said Marilla sarcastically, 'I might tell you that till now I've never been allowed to investigate an engine myself. The moment a woman lifts a bonnet, along comes a man full of ego, to demonstrate his superiority. Hundreds of women don't know a thing about engines.'

'Then they shouldn't attempt roads like this on their own. As a sex women won't admit their shortcomings.' He hesitated and she was amazed to see a dark red rising up from his throat. 'In excuse – if I *need* to excuse myself – I'll just say you happen to be the last straw in a day that's gone from bad to worse since we got up. And now—' he brought out a hand from behind his back, 'now I'm not in much of a state to fiddle round with a tiny engine!'

He had a blood-stained bandage on, very clumsily wrapped, and it looked enormous. He added: 'My men are all up at the Huts and I'm on my own with three children. I thought this must be the last of the day's calamities, but Fate had something worse in store for me – you!'

Marilla felt dismayed. 'Oh, how sorry I am. It was so thoughtless. Look, if you could tell me what to do, I'll try to dry it out under your guidance. But did one of the children bandage that? It looks so clumsy. I'm not too bad at first-aid. I'm sure I could make it neater and more manageable.'

His face was grim. 'It's not a clumsy bandage. That's swelling. It came up like a football.'

Now Marilla really was appalled. 'Then I think you must have broken a bone in your thumb. You'll have to see a doctor.'

'Yes, tomorrow. I can't go in now – too late.'

She said, 'Look, it's obvious you can't attend to my engine. Let me come in and ring a Wanaka garage to come out.'

He looked at her with some exasperation. 'You've got to be joking. A bad emergency, yes, they'd come. It's just on their knocking-off time. There and back it would be over seventy miles – and in any case, they might be finishing off urgent jobs. This is only a tiddly-winking fault – we'll get it going all right. I'll get my gear and come on down. You ought to be able to help if you don't mind soiling your hands.'

'I don't mind soiling anything,' said Marilla with conviction, 'as long as I don't hold you up too long, or have you damage that thumb any more.'

He went back into the house, shouted out some instructions, presumably to the girls, seeing it concerned dinner, and added, 'Whatever happens don't let Tony come down to help, his job is going to take him all the time there is before dark.'

By the time they reached the car, Marilla knew she wouldn't be taking the job if it were offered to her. Not after a start like this. She didn't feel like asking, but perhaps Mrs. MacGillivray was in hospital.

He certainly knew his way round an engine, and he must be almost ambi-dexterous, because he used his left hand to great effect. Or else he was just too impatient to let a woman fumble around. Suddenly she could stand it no longer and said, 'I do know how to handle a spanner, I could take that over.'

To her great surprise he let her do it. She'd thought he'd martyr himself rather than admit that a girl who could get herself into a predicament like this was capable of any sort of assistance to him. Well, it was so impressed

35

upon her mind that if ever this happened to her again, she'd know what to do, and she'd never travel round again without one of those drying sprays.

It was turning cool now the sun had dropped down behind the Alps. It was dusky, but once out on the Matukituki, it was so open there'd be light for long enough.

She helped replace everything, he slammed the bonnet down, said, 'Now get in and start her, keep your revs going to dry it completely, then when I'm satisfied it won't conk out on you again, I'll let you go. But don't stop to admire a view or pick a fern or something.'

Marilla's tone was withering. 'I'm not a complete idiot!'

She hated the way he said, 'No? But then I've had a long and disillusioning experience of people who dote on scenery and don't realize the hazards of this kind of country.'

'But I'm sure once they've met you, they'll be under no illusions about it at all. You'd put them right. And I won't be stopping to pick ferns. I don't, ever. They ought to be left in their natural habitat. And I said I was born and brought up in the mountains.'

'How old were you when you left them?'

She hated the knowing, derisive note in his voice. She flushed, but said honestly, 'Thirteen.'

He said nothing. Marilla got in, did all the necessary things, prayed for the engine to spring to purring promise, but nothing happened. Life in that dratted engine was as extinct as a *huia*. She would have felt better had he sworn long and loudly. That thumb must be giving him hell.

He spent another twenty minutes on it, and all around him the dusk deepened. Then he said crisply, 'Well, we've had it. It'll take a better mechanic than I to find the trouble. I've a real crackerjack amongst my men, but they're in a hut near that skyline over there. They won't be down till at least the day after tomorrow. I'll get a chap out from the Wanaka garage tomorrow morning, but I'm afraid it'll cost you a pretty penny. I hope you aren't like some of these girls who travel round on a shoestring.'

'I've got a perfectly good cheque-book, and my savings book, and plenty of means of identification,' said Marilla through her teeth. Then the full import struck her. 'Tomorrow morning . . . then what do I do tonight?'

She wasn't sure if it was sarcasm or humour. 'Tonight? Tonight you avail yourself of the much-vaunted high-country hospitality you seem to think has disappeared. You stay at the homestead.'

She looked aghast. He misread that. 'I may be on my own, but I assure you the children will make excellent chaperones. Anthony is twelve, Jane eleven, Anne ten.'

Marilla looked scornful. 'That never crossed my mind. I was just rueful over being such a nuisance. Giving you extra work when you've had such a day, finishing up with a nasty injury.'

'Finishing up with you,' he corrected her, then added, 'Besides, the trouble will devolve on you, not me. You can help the kids with the dinner, and make up your own bed. But first we'll have to drain your radiator. It's too much to hope, I suppose, that you have anti-freeze in?'

She agreed with him. 'It's not necessary in Wellington at this time, but I realize here that there could still be frosts.'

'Yes, it gave promise of one, with such a clear sky, though this last hour I'm not so sure. I had the glasses on Aspiring from our lantern-tower. You can just see the top from there through a cleft in the foothills. Mists were gathering. But we'll take all precautions. We won't risk cracking your cylinder head. Trouble is, these pesky cars are so tiny it's the devil's own job to get at the tap, and a dirty one.'

Marilla spread her hands out. 'They couldn't be blacker. I'll do it. My right hand will do it more quickly than your left.'

It was done, the last drops trickling out. Marilla wiped her hands on some tussock, took her duster, wiped most of the grease out, said, 'Let me clean up your left hand a little.'

How odd to be wiping the hand of a man unknown to

her an hour ago. She reached into the boot and took out her case. 'Now, don't attempt to take it from me. I've been enough of a liability.'

He conceded that, brought his left hand to cup his right elbow to ease the drag on it and trudged beside her in silence.

CHAPTER THREE

THEY went round to the back door this time, and came in to hear a girl's voice say, 'He's got some woman in trouble with a car, Tony. I only hope he can fix it for her, that's all. Wouldn't it be the end if we had to put someone up? I didn't even do many potatoes. I got sick of peeling them.'

'Well, she won't have any of mine, that's for sure. I'm just starving. Whatever happens, don't let them boil away to soup like you did last time. You should have done chips. Oh, I expect he'll fix it. Some nit who splashed through the fords at the rate of nobody's business, I expect.'

Marilla found herself flinching. Another girl's voice, younger. 'Well, *I* hope she *will* have to stay. It'd be fun. It's dull being here on our own. She could be some princess in disguise.'

A snort from the male voice. 'You and your imagination, Anne! Princesses don't drive Minis.'

'That's all you know. Princess Anne used to drive one round the grounds of Buckingham Palace. Anyway, I hope she can't get it started. I think I'll just go down and see what's happening.'

'No, you won't. You're supposed to help. That's just a dodge. You'll set the table. Just get cracking and—'

The children swung round as one when the door was pushed open and the voice of authority broke in. 'No need to go down, Anne. We *have* got a visitor, *and* she heard every word you said!'

The boy and the older girl went crimson with embarrassment.

The younger child smiled an impish smile and stuck her chin in the air. '*I* don't have to apologize. *I* said I hoped she'd have to stay. Good job Mum's not here, you wouldn't half catch it! Blue Canyon is supposed to be noted for hospitality.'

Marilla felt sorry for the other two. She grinned back

39

at the little one. 'Sorry I'm not a princess, and I *am* just a dill of a city slicker who didn't know enough to dry out her distributor after coming through the fords. And I *am* the last straw – I've already been told that. But I'll try not to make too much extra work for you. I know how you must feel.'

None of the three said a word. Youngsters always found it hard to bridge awkwardness like this. Small talk might fill the gap. Marilla said, 'You know, I expected at least one redhead, because your father's as red as I am. You must take after your mother.'

All of them burst out laughing. The boy said, 'he's not our *father*. He's our *uncle*. Our mother's as ginger as he is. We're like our father.'

Marilla, surprised, swung round on the copper-coloured uncle and said, 'Oh, I thought you were—' She stopped dead as she became aware she'd nearly said, 'Donal MacGillivray,' and added lamely, '... I thought you were the station-owner.'

'I am,' he said. 'My sister keeps house for the lot of us. Her husband is more or less my partner. They're away up in Auckland just now. But in case those potatoes go soupy again, I suggest we wash up and get ourselves sat down to our meal.'

He turned to the younger one. 'Anne, take Miss—' he stopped. 'I haven't asked your name.'

'I'm Marilla S—' some quick realization she might not now wish to reveal her identity stopped her. 'Marilla Sinjin,' she finished, using the form of her name she didn't like. Why anyone with a lovely name like St. John should wish to be called Sinjin, she didn't know, but it would serve for the time being.

'Sinjin?' asked Anthony. 'Honest Injun, is it?' and the three children shrieked with laughter at this evidence of wit.

His uncle said hastily, 'Tony, I feel we've blotted our copybook enough as it is. No comments on names. Just because you've never heard of it before isn't to say it's not a perfectly ordinary name.'

Anne's eyes lost their mirth and became rapt. 'But you are really Marilla? Fair go?'

Her uncle frowned. 'What on earth's come over you kids?'

Anne looked scornful. 'Because it's a whizz of a name for her. Don't you get it?' she said to Marilla. 'We call the house Green Gables, you see. And the new one's Lantern Hill, and we've got a Rainbow Valley – oh, wouldn't Great-granny have been thrilled?'

Marilla caught on immediately. 'Oh, I take it Great-granny was a fan of the *Anne of Green Gables* author? Well, so was my mother. She'd have liked to have called me Anne, but there were already two Annes in her brothers' families, so she called me Marilla instead.'

Jane was starry-eyed too. 'How marvellous! Great-granny called Gusty Gully Four Winds, like the harbour in *Anne's House of Dreams*, and our nanny is calling the house they're retiring to in Wanaka Ingleside. Our mum is Diana. And now we've got a Marilla.'

'Well, you won't have her very long,' said her uncle quellingly, 'so make the most of her. At the moment she needs to scrub up – Anne, on your way! Anthony, you can help me get this dirt off my left hand. The kitchen sink will do.'

Anthony had to cut up his uncle's chops too, though it didn't take much doing because Jane had casseroled them and they were as tender as chicken. The potatoes were perfect if not plentiful, so they made up for it with bread and butter. 'The pudding's just preserved apricots,' said Jane, importantly, 'but I made a baked coconut custard.'

'Goodness,' said Marilla, 'no wonder your mother's not afraid to leave you to housekeep.'

'Oh, I often have to help Mum. We all do, even Anthony. You just put some coconut in beaten eggs and milk and sugar and bake it slowly. I'll give you the recipe if you like.'

'Thank you,' said Marilla solemnly, 'I collect recipes like some people collect stamps. My mother made very sure we could all cook. She said even if we married millionaires we ought to know how, in case the tycoons took us for Pacific cruises and we got marooned on uninhabited islands.'

Anne giggled and was away. 'And you'd have to experiment with birds' eggs and coconut milk, and rub sticks together to light the fire.'

Not a glimmer of mirth reached Marilla's eyes. 'Oh, she also made us promise always to have a packet of matches in a waterproof packet next to our skin if we got shipwrecked.'

Anthony guffawed. 'But awkward if you were in a bikini when the ship went down.'

'They had to be taped to our skin, no matter what. Mother used to say no girl ought to be shipwrecked without matches and a mirror.'

Anne beamed on her. Here was a grown-up after her own heart. She liked pretending things. 'It would be lovely, wouldn't it? And you could build a tree house, with a rope-ladder saved from the wreck, and have curtains of vines and use coconut shells for dishes. What would you cook in, though?'

'Aluminium pans. It's always been a custom of the S – Sinjin family to save the pans and rope ladders first. As the bow hits the rocks, over the side they go. I mean, spearing fish on sticks and grilling them over a fire is all right for a while, but I do like a shellfish stew myself.'

Anne considered that, her pointed elfish chin in her hands. 'Yes, but sausages are nice on sticks.'

Her brother grinned, 'Well, you'd better remember to heave the sausage machine and the electric plant overboard with the saucepans.'

Jane came in quickly. 'I don't see what's wrong with chopping shellfish small, pounding it on a rock, and making sausage patties out of that. I bet if you were a castaway you'd only be too glad to vary the way you cooked things.'

Marilla decided that Jane was a pourer-of-oil on troubled waters. She looked oddly mature as she ladled out the fruit, spooned the perfectly browned custard out, offered Marilla luscious whipped cream. She had long smooth hair, acorn-coloured, tied back with a blue ribbon, a perfectly oval face, with a dimple in her chin.

Anne had a slanting fringe of dark hair across her brows, wearing that hair shoulder-length, a piquant expression that mirrored dreaminess one moment, mischief the next; Anthony had a page-boy cut of thick dark hair, well-marked brows, was tall, broad, very mature. They all had grey-blue eyes with dark lashes and an engaging sprinkling of freckles across their noses, just like her own sprinkling. These were the ages Marilla loved to teach most of all. Things weren't going too badly. They might iron out their initial clash, she and – oh, what was his name – no one had said – oh, well, she and Uncle!

Would he have a sense of humour? Would he understand if she said she felt it had been no moment to announce who she was? She couldn't say anything yet. They must wash the dishes, get that hand attended to. She glanced at their uncle and saw lines of pain etched at the corners of his mouth.

She said crisply, 'Well, let's leave our Pacific island and our shellfish stew. As soon as we've done the dishes I must look at your uncle's hand.' She gave him her first natural smile. 'I'm not too bad. I did take a course in first aid. And I'm pretty sure that whatever the damage is, a sling would ease it, it needs support.'

Jane rose with alacrity. 'We'll get these out of the way right now. Please, Uncle Rufus, don't say she can attend to it while we do them, because I don't want to miss anything.'

Her uncle looked at her. 'It's not exactly an exhibition. What a ghoul of a child! She gets practically starry-eyed over these things.'

'Well, I'm going to be either a nurse or a vet, so it's all – um – well, experience, but there's a saying.'

'All grist to the mill,' suggested Marilla. 'Well, if your uncle has no objection, I suppose you could watch, but no butting in, I want it as aseptic as possible.' Then she added, 'Rufus? Is it a nickname because of his hair?'

43

'It is not,' he said. 'Rufus has always been a family name of the Sinclairs. Our branch, anyway. I expect there's always been a lot of redheads in it, so it could have started that way.'

'Sinclair? That's your name? Well, I expect the first one was named for William Rufus. The first Sinclairs were Norman like the—' she checked. She'd nearly said, '. . . like the St. Johns.' She went on swiftly, 'Like so many families who later went up into Scotland in search of lands. Didn't a lot of them, the Sinclairs I mean, go right across the Pentland Firth to Orkney?'

Tony said, 'You're like Mum, you know things. She's very keen on the origin of names. So am I. I love family trees. Have you got a family tree? We did one for the correspondence school.'

Marilla said swiftly, not wanting too much probing, 'Not on my father's side, but we have one belonging to my mother's mother. She'd been born a Ramsay.'

'What's the clan motto of the Ramsays?'

She laughed. 'Pray and work – and right now is the time to work! Dishes, then dressings on that hand, and while we work, will someone tell me how it happened?'

Rufus told it himself, hushing down the other three voices.

'We've a pump in a shed, which gets the water up to the milking-shed. It went wrong. I got a bit careless, spun it at the wrong time and caught my hand in it. I was jolly lucky Tony was there and that his reactions are so speedy. He switched off immediately.'

The girls brought snowy white towels, laid them out on the kitchen table, produced an extremely well stocked first-aid kit. Marilla commented on it. Rufus nodded. 'We have to be well-equipped to deal with minor injuries here. At times we even have to deal with irresponsible people who get themselves marooned or injured on the mountains. Some accidents are sheer bad luck, but some are pure foolishness. Only people who don't live here, or who aren't experienced mountaineers, take this country lightly. At times, too, we have to deal with quite serious accidents

44

to ourselves. We sometimes get cut off by snow. That's when I implore the family to take all care. I don't mind if I can get the Wanaka doctor on the phone and describe the symptoms, it takes a bit of the weight of responsibility off one. Diagnosis is tricky at any time.'

She nodded. 'Marvellous to have the phone. I guess that's fairly recent.'

'Yes, Mother and Dad said Diana wasn't going to have any more babies till we had better communication. It cost the earth, of course, but it's our best friend. I'll go in tomorrow and get this seen to. It'll need an X-ray, I guess. Hope it's just a cracked bone — even so it's going to be a damned nuisance just now. But if you can make it a bit more comfy for the night I'd be very grateful.'

He laid his arm along the table, and she knew he was wincing as she took the bandages off. The swelling was a horrible sight. The flesh on the hand was torn badly too, and any manipulation wasn't going to help that.

Rufus said, 'We're always up to date with tetanus immunity, and Tony did a pretty thorough job of disinfecting it.'

'Then I won't do that again, I could re-introduce infection. Does your doctor keep you up with antibiotics to prevent that? He does? You took a pill? Well, when? Just before I arrived? Then we must time them. Now ... it's going to hurt, but has to be done. I'll be as gentle as I can.'

Three interested and slightly ghoulish faces were propped on hands, with elbows resting on the other side of the table. She could tell by the rigidity of his muscles it was hurting like hell. Marilla managed to draw two jagged tears together with plaster. They were well away from the thumb, she was thankful to find.

'I'll have to try to immobilize that thumb. Girls, have you any of those large size sticks you put in ice-blocks to make them easy to hold? Good.' They fetched them.

They had gauze finger-stalls, so she slipped these over the sticks, and got Jane to hold them in position while she immobilized the thumb first with bandaging, then with

45

strips of tough plaster. The kit yielded the sort of sling she needed, and presently the arm was securely supported. Marilla took a quick look at his face when it was over, walked across to the oil-fed stove that bubbled merrily and incessantly, and quickly made a cup of coffee from the kettle singing there. She dropped in some sugar, stirred it, brought it across to him.

He said, 'Sorry, I don't take sugar. Would you make another?'

'You're taking sugar this time, Mr. Sinclair. You need it, believe me. You're chalk-white. I don't want you passing out on me.'

He looked black-affronted. 'I've never flaked out in my life!'

'Well, there's always a first time. Now drink.'

Quite unconsciously she'd assumed her schoolmarm manner. Rufus drank, and she was relieved to see his colour return almost immediately.

Jane said slowly, 'I'm glad you're here, Marilla. I've never seen a *man* flake out before.'

'I did *not* flake out,' said her uncle irritably.

'You would have if she hadn't been there, and we'd have been scared.'

'Into the other room and let's have a bit of peace. We've missed the news, of course, but you can watch till eight-thirty. Then bed ... and by the way, it ought to be Miss Sinjin, not Marilla.'

Jane giggled. 'He's in one of his curmudgeon moods,' she observed to Anne. 'I expect he can't help it. It's reaction from his accident, to say nothing of knowing he's stuck with us on his own for a week or two. He's going to put his foot down from the start.'

Anne nodded sagely, 'Yes, but it never lasts, does it?'

Rufus said with a ferocious scowl, 'That'll do! I won't be talked over as if I'm not in the room. And I meant what I said, you mustn't call Miss—'

Anthony grinned at his uncle. 'You're fighting a losing battle. They're so carried away with the idea of her being called Marilla, and being at Green Gables, they'll call her that every second breath. Not to worry, it's only for a night.'

Rufus Sinclair made a helpless gesture and looked at Marilla. She had to own, inwardly, to an unworthy delight in seeing him bested. 'Only for a night,' she echoed. 'Let it go.'

What a glorious room their lounge was, centrally heated but with a glowing fire on too. That would be the smoke she'd seen. The firelight flickered on panelling and oil-paintings, done by Brian Halliday, one of the artists of the region. The fireplace was huge, of stones from the canyon, smoothed by the waters of thousands of years and sprinkled with mica that winked back at the light.

At the far end, curved out with a perfection that spoke of an imaginative architect, and was fairly recent, was an alcove of Alpine plants and ferns, beautifully designed. Diana's work, they told her. Centrally above it was a painting of Mount Aspiring. The children rushed across to switch on the bar lighting directly above it. The effect was exquisite. The snow seemed to shimmer. Marilla knew a moment of intense longing for Elfreda to see it.

Each side of the fireplace were deep bookshelves, filled, she guessed, with the reading tastes of Sinclairs from the time the first one had found his way here. A huge urn stood in one corner, filled with the rosetted twigs of coral japonica. It would bloom later here, than nearer the coast. Old brass and copper glinted from the shadows because there was just one set of wall lamps on. The carpet was thick and cosy.

Rufus seated himself carefully in a deep-winged armchair, resting his hand in its sling, on the arm. Anne went across and with due regard for his injury, insinuated her slim self on his knee. Marilla frowned. 'Do you think that's wise, Mr. Sinclair? She may knock it.'

'It's okay, if she stays that side. She always watches TV like this. You'll be extra careful, won't you, poppet?'

Anne nodded, snuggling down gently. She grinned her curved, impish grin at Jane. 'What did I tell you? The curmudgeon mood never lasts.'

'Now pipe down. If you're going to watch, watch dumbly, or we'll miss the dialogue.'

Unobserved, Marilla stole a look at his profile. Rugged rather than handsome, with jutting brows and an aquiline nose and square cleft chin, and with that thatch of flaming red hair, he looked decidedly formidable. Then something struck her. His profile was oddly familiar. Now how could that be? She hadn't noticed it full face.

Anthony and Jane squatted cross-legged, Jane leaning against Marilla's chair, twin of the one the owner of the Blue Canyon was occupying. A domestic scene. Suddenly, the humiliations and setbacks of the afternoon ceased to matter to Marilla. His reaction to her appearance wasn't typical, she thought. It had been born out of a series of misfortunes – to say nothing of pain.

She had a feeling that when the children were safely in bed, she would be able to confide in this redheaded man – with that colouring he'd be as impulsive as herself, so she could explain his reception had panicked her into concealing her identity. That she'd thought if he were Donal MacGillivray, her possible future employer, they'd got off to an unfortunate start and that she'd be better to look for another job. She sat on, lulled into a comfortable sureness.

Jane had said their father was in Auckland hospital, that they were going to be on their own for a week or two. He might be very glad to have a woman here to governess the children. This would be a bad time for children on correspondence lessons to have a break. So it could be he might be grateful to her after all. She could easily start now, instead of in February after the summer break.

One thing, with children so near in age, there was no dispute over staggered bedtimes. Most youngest children argued madly over their supposed right to stay up as long as the others. The girls kissed their uncle goodnight, said goodnight to Marilla, disappeared into the kitchen to make themselves hot chocolate and a snack. Tony lingered long enough to say, 'Uncle Rufus ... you'd better take some aspirin. If you've broken a bone it'll ache

48

like toothache. Mine did when I broke my arm.'

'Thanks, I will. Just switch off the TV, will you? Nothing much on now.'

'How did he break his arm?' asked Marilla.

Rufus grinned. 'His horse refused a fence, but Tony didn't. Went clean over his head and landed on a rock, unfortunately. He's game as Ned Kelly. It was broken in two places. But it was morning and we got him into Wanaka pronto.'

That reminded her. 'How are you going to drive tomorrow? I don't think I'd like to negotiate those bends with one hand out of action. You'd have no grip. You said the men won't be back tomorrow. Would you let me drive you in? I've driven quite a few cars beside my Mini?'

He looked at her consideringly. 'I *could* manage at a pinch, but I'd be very grateful if you would. The only thing would be that by the time it's fixed up, you'd be late getting back here. I expect a mechanic would come out to fix up your car earlier, but we could easily be too late returning for you to drive back to Wanaka. It could mean spending another night here. Would that interfere with your holiday plans?'

Marilla said slowly, 'I'd welcome the chance of making some return for being the last straw this afternoon. My plans are very fluid.'

He accepted with alacrity. She began to feel even more at ease. But she wouldn't burden him with her story tonight. He still looked all in. A night's sleep would make all the difference. Tomorrow he'd be refreshed and they would probably share a good laugh over her dismay – deciding she could never work for this apparently irascible Donal MacGillivray.

He said, moving his arm, and wincing, 'Just as well Diana doesn't know what's going on. There's always been some woman at the helm here. My mother and father left ten days ago for Britain. My brother-in-law, Donal, is a Canadian, and his cousin was to be in Auckland, briefly, on business, at the very time Mother and Dad were sailing. They're going to Canada by boat, then flying to

49

London. Donal decided to fly up to see his cousin. I managed to persuade Di to go with him. It took a bit of doing, but she's hoping to add to the family and knew it'd be her last chance for a bit, if it comes off, so she went. I was sure the kids and myself could manage for about five days. They were to keep up with their lessons.

'We were managing fine till today. But by last Monday we realized we'd be on our own much longer. A few hours after Donal and Diana waved Wilf off by plane, Donal was in Auckland hospital with peritonitis. They don't know a soul up there, so of course Di must stay. She wasn't worrying too much about us. She was so terrified for Donal, there was no room for panic about conditions here. They're very devoted. He's well out of the wood now, though, but it will be a longish stay in hospital. But this arm of mine has complicated things, so if you *could* see your way clear to help me with the driving tomorrow, I'd be no end grateful.' For the first time he grinned wholeheartedly, the tawny eyes glinting. 'And all I can say is praise the saints you ventured in. By the way, if we're going to be in Wanaka tomorrow I've got to get some urgent mail away. Any chance you could act as my secretary? Just one small letter really, plus an advertisement to be sent to some South Island papers.'

'Sure . . . is your writing paper in that desk? Just tell me where. The less you move that hand the better. I don't want to open any drawers with private papers in, that's all.'

He directed her, 'And bring that small table over nearer my chair and write on that. I don't want to raise my voice because the kids mustn't know a thing about this. I'll explain to my sister later when I'll have a few replies to pick and choose from. Look, the letter I must reply to is tucked safely away in my jacket on the back of the porch door – would you bring the jacket in?'

He flicked out the letter with his left hand and shook it out. 'We'll make it fairly formal, I think. This calls for that sort of treatment. Just put the date under our letter heading, would you?'

He continued: 'To Miss Eleanor M. St. John, St. Crispin's Manse, 142 Mellingham Rise, Mellingham, Wellington. Dear Miss St. John – oh, wait a moment till I explain the situation to you ...'

He needn't have said wait. Marilla's ballpoint was poised above the paper and not one word had she written. She felt as if even her breath was suspended. He was gazing in front of him.

'My sister is wanting a governess for the children to supervise their lessons. We were talking of advertising. But just before she went away, she got a ring from a friend of hers, a friend of my mother's really, from Wellington where she was on holiday. She'd heard of someone who sounded ideal for the position. Not that I took much notice – it was over to Donal and Di. But later I overheard something that made me realize she wouldn't do at all.'

Marilla felt as if her face had gone stiff, as if she couldn't frame her words properly. She looked down, mechanically wrote the address, then managed to say, 'You mean she's unsuitable for a remote spot like this?'

He gave a short, unamused laugh. 'It's worse than that. She sounds a real pill, this Eleanor St. John. A paragon of all the virtues, and, believe it or not, my precious mama and sister are planning to marry me off to her!'

Marilla dropped the ballpoint. 'Oh, surely not? I mean, would they, if they don't know her? I mean, it doesn't seem as if they *could* know her, if it was just on a friend's recommendation. Or am I wrong?' She wasn't making much sense, but perhaps he wouldn't notice that.

'I don't think they actually know her, but they know *about* her, believe me. From what I heard. It seems she has but one idea in her mind ... to marry a high-country farmer.'

She had to ask it, even if he thought she was too curious. 'And what *did* you hear?'

'Mother and Di thought I was safely up Rainbow Valley riding round the sheep. I had dung on my boots, so I came in my stockinged feet. They were going at full bore. Honestly, you never heard anything like it! This friend of Mum's must have given them all the gen. I heard Di say: "It's so ideal. He'll never guess. He shies off anyone we bring here. We were too obvious before. Once men get the faintest idea you're matchmaking, they're off. But long before we heard about this girl I said to Rufus we'd better try for a governess, so he'll never suspect. Imagine getting a girl who actually wants a high-country husband, who thinks marriage is the best career there is, who's a teacher! Why, I'm thinking correspondence lessons for her own children wouldn't daunt her at all." '

He looked sideways at Marilla and grinned. 'Talk about planning one's life for one ... they'd even got as far as plotting for my future offspring. Mother came in most enthusiastically, said, "It's been meant to be. I've always thought Rufus has been single so long he'd probably go off the deep end when he did get bitten with the love bug and marry some stupid little bit of fluff who'd have a pink fit at the isolation up here. He's just the type to be blindly besotted once he does fall for someone."

'Talk about tripe! I reckon when a chap gets over thirty he's likely to be more discriminating. They thought they had it in the bag. What sort of a girl could she be to calmly and coldbloodedly come up here with the idea of snaring a high-country husband? Can you imagine yourself doing such a thing? I ask you!'

Well, Marilla thought she'd try to answer. She said, uncertainly, 'But do you think she knew what they were planning? Mightn't she too have been an innocent victim of the matchmakers?'

'Innocent my foot! I'd never believe that. Not for a single instant. It had been discussed with them. I'm just giving you the bare bones of it. You've no idea how detailed they were.'

Marilla said, 'But I still think—'

He said impatiently, 'Look, you seem a bit biased. Your own sex and all that. And sorry, but to be quite candid I'd like to get on with this.'

She knew this was no time to explain. He was tired, cross, in pain. She said fearfully, 'So what do you intend to do?'

'Do? Tell her not to come, of course. At least tell her the position has been filled. It serves her right. Talk about a conspiracy ... do you know, I heard Mother say to Di, "Ring Brigid. She's still in Wellington. Get her to tell this Miss St. John to apply by letter, saying she'd heard through a friend we might be looking for a governess, and the friend had suggested she send along her qualifications and apply." Oh, they threw in all sorts of suggestions for good measure. Said to say she was used to solitude, that she could ride well, was never lonely and so on. And she did do just that. Here, take the letter and read for yourself.'

She had no need, but bent her head over it. She had followed so faithfully Mrs. Granville's instructions per Elfreda that it couldn't look like anything else but a put-up job. She couldn't find words at first, then, 'Why didn't you confront them there and then? They could hardly have proceeded with it then.'

'You don't know my mother and sister. They're both tarred with the one brush, as tenacious as limpets and—' his face softened, 'I love them dearly, though I don't know why! They can't get it into their heads that I'm perfectly happy as I am. Oh, I don't say I'd never get married. I admit there are a few girls who've raised my pulse rate a few degrees, but never one I'd like to spend the rest of my life with. Mother and Dad, and Di and Donal, are so happily married they can't think any other existence is worthwhile. I was as wild as blue blazes, but couldn't start a family row almost on the eve of Mum and Dad leaving for Britain. So I went off to think it out. Thought I'd surely think of some way of scotching it.

'Then out of the blue Donal's cousin rang from Canada to say he'd be in Auckland in three days' time, could Donal possibly make it? So off they all went. Di, the cunning little devil, said so casually that Brigid Granville had heard of a teacher who'd like to go governessing for a while, so she'd told Brigid to ask her to apply. When it arrived, would I either write or ring this girl saying we'd be delighted to have her, starting in the new school year in February. I thought, like heck I will!'

Marilla swallowed so loudly she thought he'd hear her. 'It – you – don't think it will disrupt the relationship between you and your sister, going over her head like this?'

'Going over her head? Well, it'll serve her right for going *behind* my *back*!'

'With what she thought were good intentions, I suppose.'

Suddenly exasperation rasped his voice. 'Look, I'm not asking your advice. I'm just dictating the flaming letter to you.'

Marilla felt the hot blood rush right up her face. 'Sorry. It was just that I thought it would be a pity if you and your sister got off-sides with each other over it.'

'We won't. We've fought royally all our lives. Di will just giggle and subside. And I'm hardly likely to quarrel with my mother on the opposite side of the world. But I can't and won't have that creature here. I couldn't possibly be natural with her. I'd begin to feel like a hunted man.'

Humiliation scorched right into Marilla. First she had had to cut and run from a surfeit of suitors and now she was accused of being a cold-blooded husband-hunter! None of it was true, yet it would effectively bar her from Blue Canyon Station ... the loveliest valley she had ever seen.

She finished writing the address, said in the best stenographer's manner, 'Yes, Mr. Sinclair?' The letter would go into Blue Canyon's private bag. It would be delivered at home. Mother or Father would stare madly at it, addressed *to* their daughter, in *their daughter's own hand-writing.* She'd have to do something about it. But what? She couldn't write here – he'd see it. The name St. John would rise up and hit him. What on earth could she do? She was committed to returning with them here tomorrow after Rufus Sinclair's thumb was attended to. Perhaps she'd be able to shake the children and Rufus off for a few moments tomorrow and ring Wellington from the post office.

The letter was finished. She wrote out the advertisement for him. He wasn't advertising in the North Island in case Di saw it. That was something to be grateful for. Imagine if Elfreda or Mrs. Granville saw it! She looked down on it. Some other lucky girl would come here. The imp at the back of her mind began to jeer. How ironic if some girl came up here and this cocksure Rufus fell madly in love with her. She could vaguely understand his mother and sister plotting. Rufus had said his mother and father were thinking of retiring soon in Wanaka. Di and Donal were moving into the new house. They'd never move Rufus from the old, she was sure of that, even by now. She thought Brigid Granville had recommended Elfreda's cousin, after seeing the programme, and had mentioned it. In fact Di and Mrs. Sinclair might even have seen it. It was obvious Rufus hadn't. They'd hoped Rufus would fall for her.

He would never believe she hadn't been party to it. It was an unthinkable position. He'd said he couldn't possibly be natural if this dame came up here! Neither, had he but known, could the dame be natural.

It was all off. Well, there were other places. She'd find one. She only wanted to get away from here without being made to look a perfect fool or a designing hussy. She hoped they'd get in to Wanaka very early tomorrow, that a mechanic might be able to come out here without delay, that she might be able to leave tomorrow afternoon or very early the morning after, and Rufus Sinclair would never know that Eleanor St. John, that paragon of all the virtues, that pill, as he had called her, had come, looked him over, and departed. A pity, in a way, that he couldn't know she wasn't in the running in the matrimonial stakes for the owner of Blue Canyon!

CHAPTER FOUR

ELEVEN had struck by the time it was finished. 'I'll make a cup of tea now,' said Marilla, 'you look all in. I'll give you the aspirin just before. What do you like with your last cuppa?'

'A slice of toasted cheese normally, and a piece of cake, but a couple of biscuits will do tonight. You must be dog-tired too, and you're finding your way round a strange house.'

Marilla laughed, 'I don't think it would exhaust me to use the pop-up toaster and grate some cheese. Do you like Marmite on it first?'

'Yes, if you can be bothered, and a sprinkle of onion salt.'

She had just browned the slices under the oven-top when the door opened and Anne appeared in a long plum-coloured nightgown with a white ruffle round the neck, that gave her the appearance of an angelic choir-boy.

Her uncle groaned. 'What now?'

She looked rather serious. 'I thought I ought to tell you I can sniff a storm.'

Marilla expected scorn from her uncle. It didn't come. He looked surprised but said, 'How come you were sniffing?'

Anne was quite matter-of-fact. 'I had a terrific dream. It will make a beaut chapter for my book, so I got up to write it down. I had to go out to the schoolroom for it. The moon was shining through the window, but it looked strange. Very white, with bars of cloud. It gave me the shivers. I thought it could give my Johanna the shivers too. I went out on to the verandah so I could see it better to describe, and I sniffed.'

Rufus stood up. 'I'll come. We didn't hear the forecast. We were doing a letter when the late one came on and we'd missed the first, of course. But—' he caught the puzzled look on Marilla's face, laughed, 'sounds incredible, but it's happened so often that we don't laugh any more. Her great-granny had it too. The first time it happened with Anne we just didn't believe it either. Not for ordinary storms, but for spectacular ones.'

Marilla found herself following them on to the stone verandah of the pioneer cottage that was joined on to the gabled house and formed a wonderful shelter for the cottage garden. Rufus had a very good pair of night binoculars. But first he stood sniffing himself. 'No feeling of snow, is there, Anne?'

The child shook her head, sniffed. 'No, it's just in the smell.'

He swept the heavens with his glasses. 'Very heavy cloud in some areas, especially Big Top. Could be some wildfire, I expect.' He turned to Marilla. 'We sometimes get electrical storms, a big downpour, very suddenly. I hope not. It could bring the fords up between the Canyon entrance and the Matukituki Road and cut us off. We never have floods here, though, all our fords drain into the Blue River in a very short distance.'

Anne said, 'What about that loose shutter on the cottage?'

'Jove, yes. We'll put the bar across. Though you and Miss Sinjin will have to do it. I couldn't. It's at the back – you've got your slippers on, so come along.'

They went to the end of the verandah, along a little path that was clearly defined in the moonlight because it was made of small quartz chips, as white as marble. The scent of hyacinths, later here, rose up to them. Bushes brushed against them as they passed, lilac, syringa, nameless sweet-smelling shrubs, planted long ago to bring a breath of the Old World into the New.

The shutter hung by one hinge. They lifted it up, secured it with the bar. Rufus said, 'Now we'll go inside and snib it.'

There wasn't the mustiness you'd have expected. This cottage must still be used, apart from the schoolroom. For the men, she found out later. It was a darling bedroom, kept exactly as it had been in pioneer days, she guessed, except for a new, luxurious carpet. The bed was sturdy, and had come from Orkney, and it was covered with a white knitted quilt and had lacy shams against the pillows. The bureau had a swing mirror on a stand, two old-fashioned white enamel candlesticks with blue rims and a crocheted cover. A sturdy Scots kist with spiralled corners and wooden knobs for handles looked as if it could hold all sorts of interesting treasures.

A strange feeling swept over Marilla. As her eyes lighted upon it, she knew almost a scalding regret that she would never be able to open those drawers and have some member of this family show her the heirlooms. There would be shawls from Shetland, surely, a christening robe yellow with age, a sash of Sinclair tartan that had adorned that pioneer Sinclair woman's white evening dress in those far Northern isles . . .

The catch was snicked and they hurried back to the warmth of the kitchen. 'You'd better warm up before you go back to bed, poppet,' said Rufus. 'I'll go and switch your blanket on again.'

Marilla took the plates of toast from the rack, began to cut them into fingers.

'Don't do that,' said Anne, 'Uncle Rufus likes his slices whole.'

'Why, for goodness' sake?'

'He likes to nibble all round the edges first,' said Anne solemnly.

Marilla stared, then burst out laughing. He didn't sound half as much of a curmudgeon. It was endearing, little-boyish.

'Right, pet. You just have a piece of mine. It'll save time. And I'm not hungry after that dinner.'

'I'm always hungry,' said Anne, biting into the toast with relish.

'True,' said her uncle, 'though where she puts it, I'm sure I don't know.'

Marilla looked down at the slim figure on the kitchen chair. 'M'm, you're certainly not the chubby type. But how heavenly for you later, not having to diet.'

'But I'm as tough as an old boot,' said Anne. 'Whipcord and muscle, that's me!'

'And brag,' said her uncle. 'Don't forget that. Now, don't settle down for the night.'

'Well, I thought I might make myself another full slice after this. I'm ravenous!'

Before she thought, Marilla said firmly, 'Oh, no, you won't. You'll get yourself so wide awake, you won't be able to sleep. Your uncle ought to have been resting long ago, but he had letters to get ready for tomorrow. Think yourself lucky you got an extra snack as it was.'

The impish grin curved Anne's mouth. 'Are you a teacher? You sound like one.'

Marilla burst out laughing. 'I am. It's not easy to shed the managing habit. I ought to have let your uncle say it.'

'I'm only too glad to have moral support. I know our Anne. She has a very alert look at the moment. It's that Johanna. If we're not careful, we'll have her telling you all Johanna's adventures from Chapter One. She's been writing that story for a year now. I reckon it'll go into five volumes or more. Now scram. Not another peep out of you. It's been some day. Just leave those few dishes, Miss Sinjin. You know where your room is.'

It was next to the girls' room. Just as Rufus left them for his room, which was upstairs, Marilla said, 'Have you an extra pillow? Be sure to put it on the side of your bed and rest that arm on it.'

'Yes, miss,' said Rufus Sinclair meekly.

Marilla was tired to death and this ache of regret sat heavily upon her. These children caught at her heart. She had loved them on sight. They would have been so interesting to teach. They would have inquiring minds, opinions of their own, and a certain philosophy and self-reliance based on their isolated life. But Rufus Sinclair would never believe she'd not been in this match-making plot. Never believe she'd not even known he existed. Might even think she'd come up here secretly to look him

59

over. And now she'd let him get as far as dictating that letter he'd be more furious than ever.

Oh, if only his mother and sister hadn't plotted! If only – stop it, Marilla. There are other remote sheep or cattle stations. Quite a few people could want a governness. You'd better do a bit of advertising yourself. That's it – give Rufus Sinclair's advertisement a week or two to draw answers, so he doesn't answer yours, and you might find yourself with a choice of districts. You might even get one in South Canterbury, near your beloved Mount Cook. She only hoped that whatever one she might get, it had no eligible bachelors around – nobody to think here was that idiotic girl on the TV programme who had said she wanted a high-country husband. Perhaps she could find out which stations still didn't have television!

The bed was warm, the pillow exactly what she liked, deep kapok, not rubber; the sweet mountain air drifted in through the little fanlight, it was only redolent of mountain heights, sheep pastures, the tang of the bush ... Marilla slid over the cloud-edges into a billowing unconsciousness.

But she woke to confusion. What on earth was going on? Never had she heard such clangour. It sounded as if the mountains were bursting asunder, shaken from their fastnesses, cracked from top to bottom by some fiendish explosion ... her whole room was lit by an unearthly glow, green and yellow and malevolent. Then as she sat up, terrified, the whole room blacked out, only to be lit again the next moment by a sulphurous light. What on earth could it be? She sprang out of bed, clutched at an apricot dressing-gown, huddled it about her, rushed to her window.

The whole sky was illumined with a blinding glare, Anne's electrical storm playing Old Harry with this pocket of the mountains. It was situated just a little east of them, and south.

There was a rush of feet and the three children erupted into her room, one of them snapping on the light. Nothing less scared could be imagined.

60

'What did I tell you?' Anne was demanding.

Jane's eyes were starry. 'Wait till we tell Mum 'n' Dad! This is the worst I ever remember!'

Anthony, rushing to the window, said, 'Oh, beaut . . . look at that one . . . lemon-yellow and fluorescent green. Whacko, just watch it – it's just like searchlights!'

Their uncle appeared at the door, his red hair on end. 'Now look what you've magicked up, young Anne! What damage this'll do. Miss Sinjin, you're having quite a night. Aren't you glad now you're a city bird? You don't get them as violently as this in Wellington – look at those lights, over the Witchpot.'

Marilla said, 'No, in Wellington, we only get the roofs blown off houses. No fireworks.' Her teeth were chattering a little. It was terrifying, even though something in her exulted in the spectacle. 'Do you often get them like this?'

'I never remember one on so large a scale, and I've lived here all my life. I only hope to heaven it stops soon and doesn't bring down our telephone or power lines.'

It seemed incredible such a storm should be playing itself out over the mountains, yet there was not a breath of wind, only the atmospherics making merry hell with lights and noise. The sound was indescribable. It was tossed back from gorge to gorge, peak to peak, ravine to ravine, caught now in the river-beds and hurled upwards to splinter into a myriad fragments of crystal sound, then, unbelievably, gathered together again to volley and thunder in the mighty acoustics of the area.

'And they talk about breaking the sound barrier!' said Rufus Sinclair, standing erect, as if bracing himself against the impact.

Suddenly the usually composed Jane turned and buried her face against Marilla. 'I – I – I don't like it any more,' she said. A split second later Anne moved nearer, slipped a hand in hers, and even Anthony fell a little silent.

It reached a screaming crescendo, all the more eerie because they knew it wasn't the whistle of wind. There was one more clap, then a silence descended as if earth was holding its breath. Then into that pool of stillness roared the sound of the heaviest rainfall Marilla had ever heard, as if it was pounding the iron roof with the hammers of the devil's anvil. It was no use speaking. They couldn't have heard each other. Rufus turnèd and motioned them all out, Marilla included, shepherding them into the kitchen. He did something to the stove with his left hand so that it blazed into quicker heat, pulled the kettle on. Evidently he thought they needed something for their shattered nerves. He indicated to the girls to get out the china.

They spooned instant coffee into big mugs, set a huge tin of home-made ginger snaps on the table. They sat round, drinking, waiting for the storm to subside.

'It's a cloudburst,' said Rufus Sinclair.

Conversation was now carried on in intense whispers, pitched to penetrate below the drumming.

Marilla leaned forward to Rufus. 'We won't get out tomorrow, will we? Those fords between us and the Matukituki Road will be too deep for fording, won't they?'

He nodded, looking at his watch. 'It's already tomorrow, Miss Sinjin, if such a thing can be. It's three o'clock. You're dead right. Besides which, even on the Matukituki, there'll be washouts. I'm afraid yesterday's adventure has stonkered your holiday. You're holed up here with us.'

'I wasn't worrying about that. I was thinking of your thumb. You need medical aid.'

He nodded. 'Yep. Oh, well, they endured worse in the old days. I daresay it'll come right, though I'd hate to get a permanently stiff hand out of it.'

'I shouldn't think it'd be permanent. Even if it set a bit crookedly, they can do wonders with modern surgery.'

He nodded. 'One thing I'm glad of . . . we've got our shearing done.'

An hour later the noise was abating. It was still raining heavily, but not as if clouds had crashed together and emptied. The children began to nod and were sent to bed.

Rufus Sinclair said when they were away, 'I'm going to dress. I'll have to be out at first light to inspect damage – I didn't dare say so in front of them or they'd be all for staying up too. Would you like to go back now and try for some sleep?'

She looked at his face. Under its ruddiness it was drawn with pain. 'I think I ought to be round to make you the occasional coffee if nothing else. I don't like the look of you.'

They both laughed at that. Rufus said, 'I don't blame you – I've never regarded myself as exactly hand-some. Maybe that's why Mother and Di are so desperate to get me off! It's been quite a relief to let myself go to you, Miss Sinjin.'

She thought: Uh-uh . . . if only he knew!

He continued, 'I'll make an inspection of the rooms from time to time. By the sound, the guttering's still not coping, it's pouring over. If we keep an eye on danger spots, we may save a bit of damage from water, down the walls. One bit of pine-branch washed down a spout and blocking it could do hundreds of dollars' worth of damage to the papers. Mother redecorated before leaving.'

He said, idly, after a pause, 'I hope this storm doesn't get reported overseas. Don't suppose it will, but I don't want the parents knowing any alarm. They're visiting Donal's people in Canada first, then going across to my other sister's, whose husband is a doctor doing post-graduate study in London. Kathleen loves London, but was naturally a bit homesick, so Mother thought if she had a visit from them, she wouldn't feel it was so far. Regarding Lantern Hill, Di and Donal move across any day now, the carpets are down, and only the curtains to be finished and the furniture arranged. It arrived just before they left. It's just standing there. Di said not to place it, she wants the fun of it herself.' He scowled. 'That's why Mum and Diana cooked up this hideous plan of the husband-hunting Eleanor. Well, I must get into something more suited for going outside later, in case I have to clear drains.'

She rose too. 'Don't be too proud to sing out for help if you can't get into your shirt. That hand's so huge with swelling and splints and bandages, the cuff won't go on easily. I could do it very gently.'

She returned to the kitchen, very workmanlike in checked trews and a big natural wool sweater with a fair-isle yoke, pulled over them, and sturdy brogues. She'd tied her bright hair back tightly with a length of royal blue ribbon.

He was standing at the table in vest and trousers, a dark plaid shirt in his hand – coat style, fortunately. She took it from him, held it behind him. 'Put the injured hand in first. It won't drag so much.'

The cuff wouldn't go over at all, even so. She slipped it off, picked up some scissors, snipped the seam. 'That will go on now. I guess the slightest touch is excruciating.'

He nodded, watching her. She got it on him, kept her face very serious as she tucked his shirt into his waist-band. Thank goodness he didn't know who she was. He'd think all this devoted attention a means to an end. 'I know you could have left your shirt out, but it's not going to be exactly tropical outside, later, and loose shirts are much colder. Have you some sort of a sleeveless pullover?' He directed her to the porch where a sturdy jerkin hung.

She noted that he was glad to sit down. But shortly he went into the summer kitchen and returned with a large book on medical matters. He said, 'I've a feeling this isn't a break. I've had a fair experience of those. I've come to the conclusion it's dislocated. If so I'm going to attempt to get it back. There'll be no show of seeing a doctor for two or three days, and I'm going to be worse than useless. Now don't say I oughtn't to touch it. I wouldn't if there was any chance of seeing someone with the know-how.'

Marilla held her tongue, though she wondered if he had any idea how painful it was going to be. She con-tented herself with saying, 'Well, if the bleeding starts up on those other bits, I'm here to bandage it.'

'Thank the Lord you don't appear to be the sort to go into the vapours! I may have been rough on you this afternoon, but I could have done a lot worse.'

She ignored that, though conscious she felt pleasure in it. She said, 'Once you get hold of it, if it's broken, I think you'll know. Manipulate it very gently at first, and if there's any feeling of grating, I think you'd better desist.'

Well, he was sensible, not cracking too hardy. She loathed men who tried to appear impressively tough in front of women. She unwound the bandages very gently, removed the splints. It was a nasty sight, congealed, bruised, swollen.

He fingered it carefully, was able to move it a little, said, 'Better look away, it mightn't be a nice sight. I'm going to pull it out a little, then try to slip it back in.'

'I won't look away. It could be good experience. Teachers are usually within reach of medical aid, but you never know.'

'You're as ghoulish as the children.' He was easing it out; he said, 'Well, here goes . . .' thrust, gave an agonized cry and the next instant had slid to a heap on the floor from his chair.

Marilla echoed his cry, flopped to the floor beside him, turned him over, off his hand. She pulled herself together. It was just extreme pain that had caused this reaction. He'd had all he could bear. He'd be round very soon.

Then it hit her. She knew what she must do. But dared she? Well, he'd been trying it himself. She cautiously, and with a terrified feeling, picked up his hand. She could feel for a broken bone better than he could, while he was out to it. There didn't seem any grating, any loss of rigidity which would indicate a clean break, and she thought it did feel dislocated.

She set her teeth, took a firm grip, pulled it a little towards her, then pushed it back. There was a click, and she was practically sure it had gone in. Then she felt slightly sick. What if she had done irreparable damage to the tissues or sinews or whatever was there? Now she must try to bring him round. She ought to raise him up, then try to get his head down . . . but how? Like his small niece, he was all whipcord and muscle, but thick-set as well as being over six feet. It was like trying to move the rock of Gibraltar.

She slid her left arm under his shoulders, slightly raised him. Oh dear, that was no good. His head was lolling horribly. She brought her arm up round his neck. That low, hard-seated knitting chair was fairly near. If she could heave him on that, she could then thrust his head down between his knees. That would bring him round. *If* she could.

His head fell against her, his hair rough beneath her chin. She gave a terrific heave. The next moment his voice said, 'What's happening?'

Marilla slackened her grip a little, turned her face. His was an inch from hers. The reddish-brown eyes were trying to focus. Then they did. It was a strange moment. He looked so puzzled. She had a feeling that when he'd blacked out he'd completely forgotten this nuisance of a stranger. Emotions struggled on his features.

Then she saw recognition dawn. 'Oh, lord,' he said ruefully, 'I *did* pass out. Hell's bells! Now it's all to do again.'

She shook her head. 'No, I shoved it back while you were out to it. I just hope I've done the right thing.'

It took a moment or two for it to sink in. He probably wasn't fully conscious, because he stayed there, as he was, his head against her shoulder, as she knelt on the rag mat. He closed his eyes. She said urgently, 'Rufus, don't flake out on me again, at least not till I get you on this chair.'

His voice was slow, blurred. He couldn't know what he was saying. 'Oh, I don't know. This is very nice. What's a chair got to offer in comparison?'

Her voice sounded distracted. 'Oh, dear, now he's light-headed! Rufus! You've got to help me. I've tried pushing and heaving. Do you hear me? You've got to help yourself on to that chair, then if you go out to it again, I can thrust your head between your knees. Now ... up you go!'

'Sounds horrible,' he muttered. 'Who wants to be thrust?'

In spite of her anxiety, Marilla laughed. Then she pulled herself up. 'It's no laughing matter, Marilla,' she said out loud. 'He doesn't know what he's saying. Rufus! I'm going to heave now whether you like it or not!' and she gave him a preliminary shake.

The schoolmarm voice did it. He put his good hand on the floor, turned with his weight on it, and with her help, pushed himself up and on to the chair. She stood there panting. He kept his eyes shut. She closed in on him and put her hands at the back of his head. One moment it was limp, the next it wasn't. He resisted her. 'All right,' he said. 'I'm round. I *won't* be thrust.'

She giggled weakly with relief. He leaned back, opened his eyes, said, 'Did you really say you'd got it back into its socket?'

'If that's what you call it, I think I did. It clicked. How does it feel? No, don't move it, you might pass out again.'

But she was too late. However, he could waggle it freely.

'You've done it, girl, good for you! It's damned sore, but the pain was excruciating before.'

She made some more coffee, sugared again, to his disgust. 'Now, no moves against my holding it for you. Your reflexes will be limp at the moment. You might drop the mug and scald yourself. Now sip.'

'Yes, teacher,' said the redoubtable Rufus Sinclair meekly. His good hand came up to steady the mug, closing over hers. The rain had settled into a steady downpour. He told her to take a chair, began to talk of like happenings. Marilla let him. It would take his mind off his injury, and she thought it might be good for that joint to be free of trappings for a time. She put a cushion on the arm of a more comfortable chair and got him into it and, to his further derision, put his feet on a hassock she'd noticed in the lounge.

'What a fusspot! Worse than Mother! Never did I think I'd be made to rest propped up on my grandmother's hassock.'

'They're wonderful boons. Can't think why they ever went out of fashion. You might be able to doze, propped

67

back by that, with your head against the wing. You'll be all the better able to cope with what you have to do when daylight comes if you have a little sleep now.'

He submitted. 'If I do drop off, will you wake me in an hour's time? I must signal the men from the lantern tower then.'

'Yes, I'll keep an eye on the rooms for leaks.'

He was asleep almost before she was out of the room. There was only one leak. It was down the corner of a small porch, painted, not papered, so it wouldn't matter so much. She guessed that it was where a storm-water drain led off the roof. She flung a towel in the corner to take the water, donned an anorak from the back porch, pulled the hood over her head, and took a torch outside with her. It took just a moment to see that leaves had been washed down the pipe and had formed a solid mat against the grating it drained into.

She need not wake Rufus. She cleared them away, forced her fingers up, found a plug of leaves in the bottom two inches and the next moment water was deluging her feet.

She tiptoed back, took off her socks, put them on the rack to dry and donned slippers. She woke him promptly on the hour, pointed to his hand. 'Look, Mr. Sinclair, the swelling's been going down noticeably, all the time, so we must have done the right thing.'

He was greatly relieved and grateful. 'Good. Wrap it up and then I'll have to get you to come with me. It's a tower over the stables, built by the first Sinclair here. It gives us a good view of Mount Aspiring one way; a tiny glimpse of the lake through another gap, on the right of that.'

She strapped up the hand again, said to him, 'If you thrust it into your jacket, it will take the weight off. It will still ache, you know.'

He gave her an oil-slicker, a sou-wester, boots. 'We have most sizes up here.' Marilla tucked her trews into big farm socks. He had a very powerful torch. By the light of it she was able to pick her way over unfamiliar territory. A dog barked, was silenced.

The stable smelled warm. It was stored with hay. A

wooden staircase led up to the tower. It was quite near the new house.

'I expect that's why they called it Lantern Hill?'

'Yes, and the fact that Jane wanted it called that. Anne has always been able to say she was *Anne of Green Gables*, now Jane can be *Jane of Lantern Hill*. I suppose you've read that one too? As a matter of fact, it was my own favourite.'

Marilla was conscious of pleasure. She was glad he had read L. M. Montgomery's books – her own brothers had too.

As they came into the four-square windowed turret where a strongly-lensed lamp, electrically lit, hung from the domed centre, she had a curiously familiar feeling sweep over her as if she'd been here before. Then it hit her. This was the original of one of the drawings in Elfreda's children's books. Fancy, all through the years they had thought those drawings purely imaginary. Poor Elfreda – that had been her secret. She must have hugged it to herself.

'That window, the one that gives us the glimpse of the lake, also shines down the Canyon Road. It's a grand sight on a wild night if we've been out at some dance in Wanaka or Queenstown. If anything like this occurs when any of us are up in one of the huts, it's a rule to check before daylight, to make sure all is well. That's Number Three Hut. You can see they've put a hurricane lamp in the window, expecting me to contact them. They won't have slept much, anyway. The top man – there are bunks – would be about three feet under an unlined tin roof. The rain would sound like a cannonade.'

There was a round, scratched table under the big light. He pulled a chair across to it, mounted it, put down his good hand to her. 'You can take two corners of the piece of three-ply I use to blot out the light with.'

It was fascinating, primitive, effective. They got their reassuring flashes. Everything okay there and here.

Half an hour after they got back to the house the darkness began to grey and the rain ceased altogether.

CHAPTER FIVE

Much to Marilla's surprise the dawn came in with splendour, flinging banners of coral and rose over a sky that was a pale green, tipping the crystalline peaks with amethyst and amber and gold, and lighting up a hundred waterfalls and cascades that yesterday hadn't existed. As if nature was trying to recompense for her mood of the hours of the night.

'This will loosen a lot of snow,' said Rufus, at the window. 'It's been clinging to the rock faces, but now it will be washed off. I heard crashes through the night. Although one seemed to come from the Canyon direction. Very like an avalanche, though, so it must have been the acoustics – an echo, banging against the Canyon walls.'

'Will you have bad stock losses? It seems terrible to even admire the sunrise when it may have brought disaster to hundreds of sheep and cattle.'

'We may have lost a few, but not as in heavy snowfalls. Our land is well drained and the animals seek shelter. Here, where there's so little level ground, rain doesn't do much damage to stock. But there'll be plenty to keep us busy. Thank heaven you got my thumb back, Miss Sinjin. It's little short of a miracle we've still got power and phone, but any time it could be cut, undermined by water. There was no gale with this, or we'd have lost contact long ago. I'm going to get through to Wanaka to report this, and if you'd like to ring your people and say it could be that you might be out of touch by mail for a few days, you'd be very welcome to do so. It can alarm parents if they don't know where a daughter is. I guess we'll be able to get through the fords out towards the Matukituki Road in a day or two as long as they've had no major damage there, but then you've still to get your car fixed. You should let someone know.'

Marilla felt frozen. What could she say to her people if

he remained within hearing? They'd ask her questions about being already at this homestead she'd applied to, would assume she'd made herself known – oh, dear, and she mightn't be able to fob them off with non-committal replies!

He reported to Wanaka on the state of things at Blue Canyon, asked about any other news that might have come through, of other affected areas, but none was available yet; then he decided to send a telegram. Marilla stiffened when she realized it was to Miss St. John, regretting that the post had already been filled. He sent another longer one to his sister saying if news of a spectacular storm reached them, not to worry, they were safe and well.

He turned to Marilla. 'I'm off to look at that shutter. Would you like to get your phoning done while I'm doing that? And,' he smiled, 'don't reverse the charges, I reckon I owe you the price of a call to Wellington, for setting my thumb joint.'

As soon as the door closed Marilla flew to the phone, but to ring Elfreda, not home. Elfreda must know the set-up here, and it was her friend who'd engineered the whole thing. Elfreda could let Mother know a wire from the homestead was on its way and why. A heaven-sent opportunity, this.

It was wonderful to get through so quickly. How odd, when with the aunts, Elfreda had always been vague and dreamy, but now she was crisp and quick in the uptake.

Marilla said, 'Elfreda, I want to talk fast because I dare not be overheard. I'm at Blue Canyon, and a storm has cut us off from Wanaka, but they don't know who I am. Let me explain very quickly, and you can comment at the end in case Rufus Sinclair comes back in.' She explained, added, 'I don't think we'll be cut off for long – it will be only because of the fords in the valley, but Mr. Sinclair thinks the phone lines may collapse. He suggested I ring home. I'm afraid Mother would demand far more details, and I dare not get copped. I want to get away from here as anonymously as I came. I never want to clap eyes on

Rufus Sinclair again. So would you explain to Mother? But not in the hearing of the aunts. Slip out to a phone. Tell Mother she mustn't ring here, that I'll ring her from Wanaka when I've escaped.'

'Will do, Marilla – what gorgeous fun!'

'Fun! It's been hellish.'

Elfreda ignored that. 'What did you think of Blue Canyon?'

She had to be honest. 'It's like another world. Like something left unspoiled when the rot set in on earth. Untouched.' She heard a sound, said, 'Well, here's Mr. Sinclair. He'll want his breakfast. I should have said to you there are three fairly big children here besides him.' She heard him chuckle, realized it sounded as if she were reassuring a shocked mother she wasn't cut off alone with the station-owner, said hurriedly, 'They're lovely children, Anthony, Jane and Anne. So don't worry about me. I'll be back in Wanaka as soon as the fords are down and my car is fixed. Then I'll wander down to the more southern lakes. What did you say? Oh, might you? That would be marvellous. Yes, I'll be at Wanaka for a few days before I take off. Now I must go. Bye-bye.'

She turned to face him. 'Now breakfast, and that quickly. Is it porridge, with bacon and eggs to follow?'

'Yes – ah, here come the kids, tumbling over each other to get here. Now look, bunch, straight into the bathroom, no skipping your washing.'

Anthony frowned, 'Oh, gosh, I thought it'd be a case of getting out as soon as possible, Uncle Rufe.'

'Scram! Washing takes only half the time it takes to eat and I can't see you skipping that.'

'You can just put the dishes in the washer, and leave bedmaking till later,' Rufus decreed after breakfast. 'I want you all outside, including Miss Sinjin.'

'Bit stupid to keep calling her that when she's got to pitch in and help,' said Anthony.

His uncle nodded. 'Fair enough. Another cup of tea, please, Marilla of Green Gables. And make it Rufus.'

She laughed. 'Couldn't I make it Matthew? That's

72

what Marilla's brother was called. Rufus sounds more like Windsor Castle and the New Forest than Prince Edward Island in the St. Lawrence.'

Their shout of laughter startled her. Three fingers pointed at their uncle. 'He *is* Matthew! Rufus Matthew.'

'He looks more like a Rufus, though, with a thatch like that.' Rufus said, 'Well, if ever there's a case of the pot calling the kettle black, that's it!'

'Not black, red,' said Anne through a mouthful of toast. 'Gosh, aren't we witty this morning? Did your brothers call you Carrots, Marilla? Have you got brothers?'

'Yes, two. They called me Ginger.' She laughed. 'I hadn't been called it for years till a fortnight ago. I was in a bus beside an open window, and a youngster was playing on the footpath. He looked up, pointed a finger and yelled, "Yah! Ginger!" The whole busload looked shocked at his cheek, then the next moment we were all laughing because he was as ginger-headed as I am!'

'You couldn't call that beautiful shade ginger,' said Rufus. 'Now I'm pure ginger, but you're copper.'

Tony said, 'I think it's exactly the shade of the rump of a Hereford with the sun on it.'

They all collapsed. Then Marilla said, 'I take it as a compliment – Herefords are my favourites. Now let's get out. City slickers aren't allowed to gum up the works with small talk.'

The ground was sodden, but as they emerged into the stable yard they all stopped, enchanted by the enhanced beauty, with every leaf on every tree shining silver and crystal. The rocks were diamonded, winking back colour, the whole air seemed vibrant with the sound of running waters and above it rose birdsong.

Suddenly Marilla shivered. 'Just as well you've such splendid natural drainage, with the two rivers. It would be ghastly otherwise, pent up in a valley.'

'Yes, I think old Magnus, the first Sinclair here, knew what he was about. We've had minor landslips, of course, after torrential rain, but it would take a mountain to fall to block these outlets. Tony, there's a bit of trouble, over there, see?' Two carcasses, sodden and pathetic bundles of wool, were hauled out of the stream where a couple of ewes had perished, washed down from higher up. But there were very few casualties. Mountain sheep were hardy.

They worked hard, all of them, came back, had coffee and biscuits, then set out again, this time taking the road that led towards Wanaka. 'There's a gulley in there, well back, leading off the road,' said Rufus. 'I'd like to see how the cattle are up there. Not that I anticipate any trouble, but I'd like to make sure. It may be rough going, once we leave the car, because it's bound to be somewhat scoured out, so we'll take it easy. No-one is to scramble ahead.'

Marilla drove under Rufus's guidance till they reached the gulley.

'Horo Gulley is beyond this lead-in one. The gulley proper and its stream run into the Waihemo, away from the Blue River.'

'What does Horo mean?'

They laughed. 'Landslide. It's supposed to have a fault running through it; every now and then it loosens a bit, but it never does any real harm. It's the only unstable ground round here.'

Tony said, 'Which doesn't mean a thing. Because our terrain is like the Rock of Gibraltar. Our biggest slips are just little ones.'

His uncle groaned. 'Don't, Tony. Sounds like famous last words!'

They worked round the shoulder of the hill, single file, on a narrow sheep-track that avoided the stream that yesterday had been a dry bed.

Marilla said, 'I've not even seen the Waihemo River yet. It runs down the edge of the far hills, doesn't it? Hemo ... doesn't that mean disappearing? I've just started taking Maori lessons so that I can teach it later. The Disappearing Water ... because it can't be seen from the homestead valley, perhaps?'

'Not really, though it's a good try. That name usually means water disappearing in the river when the tide is out, so it's more likely to be used for rivers near the coasts. But the Waihemo doesn't even run into Lake Wanaka, much less the sea. There's a legend that long, long ago the Waihemo disappeared and that the little lake it goes to nearly dried up. Then suddenly the waters flowed back.'

'Have you ever been to the little lake?'

'Just once. Dad and I and a couple of mountaineers did it. We had to live hard, but it was worth it. Primeval forest almost. Remote, and untouched. I've always dreamed I'd like to do it again but never seem to get the time. Tony, give Marilla a hand. This is steep and slippery. I can't, with one hand out of commission. Cling to those fuchsias.'

The native fuchsias were gnarled and strong and got them up the last steep bit to turn the corner and meet the sunlight again. The girls were beside their uncle, enjoying having to steady him occasionally. They reached the top first, with him, and something in the stillness of their stance as they did so riveted Tony and Marilla's attention. They stepped up beside them. Tony said, 'My God!' and for once went unrebuked.

To the others it was more startling than to Marilla, for this was terrain she'd never seen before. Then Rufus Sinclair said slowly, 'It's gone. Not just Bastion Hill, but the river. It's just gone.'

Marilla took a quick look at him. His face was blanched, his eyes had a look of shock. He pulled himself together, swept his glance north, south, east, searching, assessing, trying to take in what was too immense to take in.

Anne shivered violently. 'I don't like it. It's always been there. Where's it gone?'

'Aye.' Rufus's tone was grim. 'That's the question. Where's it gone? All that water, eating its way down, undermining God knows what. This was what I heard. If that downpour hadn't been so loud I'd have known it was a landslide, a cataclysmic slip.'

Jane said, 'Uncle, how can we find out where it's gone?'

Marilla was amazed at Jane's practical acceptance. But

then these were children of the wilderness, they had always lived with the hazards of nature, were used to relying on themselves.

Rufus turned to Marilla. 'The Waihemo came snaking in from there ...' he pointed, '... and then turned sou'west, avoiding Bastion Hill, sweeping round by its contours, only,' his voice shook a little, 'Bastion Hill is gone. That's where it was ... that disaster area.'

It was horrible to see, the big cliff that hadn't been there yesterday, exposed in all its raw, new nakedness, as if a knife, forged in some monster's smithy, had sliced it down. No softening tussocks clung there, no alpine plants, not a single tree.

The trees that had once crowned the top were flung in tangled and shattered heaps amid tons of rocks, rubble, clay, filling the entire gully and, evidently, cutting off the river that had run there, unconfined.

Suddenly Rufus said, 'One way we can try to discover what's happened to the river is to listen. Anne, you'll pick it up better than any of us. With all this surface water still streaming off the hills, we ought to be able to trace the force of water that's got to go somewhere. If not, we'll have to scramble up to a higher vantage point than this.'

They strained so hard to listen; it almost hurt their ears because the birdsong was so deafening. Anne picked it up a second or two before them. It seemed so strange, that slim slip of a child, her sudden prick of awareness; she pivoted and pointed with tiny forefinger, back towards where, could they but have seen it, the Blue Canyon Road would be.

Rufus said, 'Oh, it can't be. That'll be the increased volume in the Blue you're hearing.'

Then they fell silent again, straining. Then Rufus nodded. 'You could be right. It's slightly more east than the Blue.'

He put out a hand to restrain Tony's instinctive rush. 'We'll take it easy, mate. We don't want to start a hillside moving – though perhaps it's settled. I've got to see where it's going, all that water, then beat it back to make a report. It's going to be horribly near our telephone poles, so the sooner I make it the better. You can all come, but no larking about – I'd rather you were under my eyes, and if I shout stop, you stop dead. Savvy?'

They savvied. The magnitude of the happening had subdued them all. Then Tony said, 'It's almost certainly made its way to the Blue, hasn't it, Uncle?'

His tone was grim. 'Yes. There's a faint hope it may have diverted through Leap Frog Gulley, but I doubt it.'

Marilla said, 'Wouldn't that solve the problem . . . if it went into another river? I mean it couldn't bank up that way.'

He looked at her, working his way along the hillside. 'It's no use wrapping it up, I'm afraid. If it has, it will have swept the road away.'

Twenty minutes later, silent, anxious, full of dread, they came to a shoulder of the hill and stopped dead. The Waihemo was in sight, its waters, still being fed by the countless watersheds, was a mass of foaming, leaping water, tumbling great rocks and trees over like toys, gashing through what yesterday had been a fold of the hills round which the road had curved quite gently.

Now no one could describe it as a fold, as a gentle curve. It was a narrow gorge and the road just didn't exist any more. Each edge hung over, undermined to a thin jagged crust. There would never be a road there again, just a bridge, a bridge that would be a feat of modern engineering, because there were no natural approaches and the Canyon, receiving these new waters, was far below.

Marilla kept quiet. It wasn't the moment for a stranger to comment. There was no chance of lightening a situation with a philosophical approach. It was a catastrophe, no less.

She wondered if Rufus's feelings might have been relieved had he sworn long and loud. He just said very quietly, 'I think we've solved the mystery of the legend. I'm inclined to think this is its original course, then an earthquake must have diverted it to flow south and west.

I'm no geologist or seismologist, but I'm inclined to think this will have stabilized the fault. But future benefits, if any, can't be considered in the light of what may be happening downstream. This, pouring into the Blue, and therefore into the Matukituki, is going to flood an enormous tract of country. We've got to get back to get an alert going to prepare everyone for it, before those telephone poles go.'

They all looked up at them, silhouetted against the skyline of the far hill, their frail link with the outside world.

'Of course some damage will have been done by now. The flats in the Matukituki Valley will be flooded, the road will have wash-outs, and there'll be stock losses, but they won't guess at this, and engineers must be warned that a permanent volume of water will be going into the Matukituki and eventually into the lake.'

They wasted no time on the way back, piled into the Rover. Rufus even had a word of praise for Marilla: 'You may not know much about a car's innards, but you're a good driver.'

She was impressed with the way the little girls, even, wasted no breath on bemoaning how they'd be cut off, till Rufus had made all his contacts. They could tell by his answers and his face that the situation was already serious. He hung up, turned round.

'The Motatapu area caught it too and that bridge is gone. And the bridge over the Matukituki has been swept into the lake. That cuts off the West Wanaka Station folk, though they'll always have some access down lake. They're on the shore, Marilla. They didn't hear a thing. It must have been a terrible shock to wake up and find that bridge gone. Well . . . coffee. Lots of coffee. All I can say is thank the powers that be you got my thumb back last night. Now, kids, we're on our own. Everyone's got to be very obedient, and above all, take no risks. We want no accidents. You heard me tell the Kingfords to let your mother know. By now I'm mighty glad your father developed appendicitis up there. Nice if it had happened here after the road went. Oh, before we have that coffee, Marilla, ring your people and let them know you're pent up here indefinitely.'

This time she had an audience. She rang Elfreda again. Luck was with her once more. Elfreda said, 'I had a feeling it might be you and rushed to the phone.' She listened till Marilla got the whole story out. Marilla was careful not to call her by her unusual name. It wasn't likely, but Rufus's mother and sister might have mentioned the contact Brigid Granville had had, when they were discussing their matchmaking, and after all, Elfreda had been here long ago.

Elfreda said, 'Right, Marilla, I'll let them know. What a wonderful adventure! I'd give ten years of my life right now to be in your shoes, holed up at Blue Canyon.'

Could this be Elfreda? Elfreda went on, 'Don't worry about a thing. What fun being incognito; some folk have all the luck. I won't let your people worry. It's not as if I don't know where you are and who you're with.'

'Who I'm with?' cried Marilla unguardedly, and hoped, next moment, she hadn't given anything away.

Elfreda laughed. 'Rufus was a gorgeous redheaded imp when I was there, and as self-reliant as any boy of that age could be. They breed them tough up there. Here's hoping they don't throw a bridge across that chasm for months. You'll have the time of your life there, Rilla. Good-bye.'

Marilla found herself staring at the mouthpiece of the phone quite stupidly before replacing it. The four pairs of eyes regarding her looked as if they expected her to say something. She managed to get out, 'Thank goodness for a family not likely to flap! Mother fusses a bit, in the nicest possible way, but even she isn't likely to get het up. My father's cousin simply said that I'd have the time of my life, that I had a job to do, so get on with it. That teachers can even teach in the outback.'

Jane said flatly, 'Then we won't get out of anything, after all!'

'You certainly won't,' said her uncle. 'You don't know

79

how lucky you are. Your lessons could have fallen back badly.'

'Lucky!' said Anthony. 'I could think of another name for it.'

A small hand crept into Marilla's. Anne's. The small pixie face looked up into hers. 'I'm glad you're here. I don't like it much when there's nothing but men around.'

Marilla felt a strange sensation . . . warmth, a tug at the heart, something purely maternal, she supposed. Jane, now, would probably be more sufficient, in which she was wrong.

Jane said, with great fervour. 'So'm I. It's the cooking. Mum's seen to it we can all cook a snack, even Tony, but she's always been here to time things for us. We had a girl working here one shearing-time, helping in the shed. Said she didn't want to help in the kitchen. She was having a working holiday round New Zealand and had been helping in the kitchens of tourist hotels. Said she didn't know why, but cooks or chefs as a breed were all bad-tempered. We thought that was funny because our mum loves cooking, but since we've been on our own, I know why. It's getting everything cooked by a certain time and not burning anything or having things go soggy, and keeping about five things warm at once and then,' her voice took on a tone of disgust, 'Tony saying "What went wrong with this?" Men!'

Marilla burst out laughing. 'You've forgotten one thing, poppet, for me it's always the last straw. That's getting the men to the table at the precise moment you want them. My dad's the limit. He's been known to say anxiously, because the tablecloth's not on, "I hope you've remembered I've got kirk session tonight," so we rush like billy-o, and as we slap the plates of food on the table we discover he's missing and he's either deep in some book in the study and sings out, "Just start without me," or he's decided to ring the organist. We sure do have trouble with that man!'

Rufus said, 'Oh, is your father a minister too? Goodness, we do seem to be mixed up with daughters of the clergy just now, don't we?'

Marilla bit her lip. Jove, she'd have to watch her small talk. On subjects you knew were tricky, it was easy to be guarded. Now, any moment, he'd say, 'Oh, and you're in Wellington. Do you know this St. John family?'

But he didn't. He was having trouble of his own. Because Jane said curiously, 'What do you mean, Uncle Rufe – what other minister's daughter do we know, except our own? And she's only my age.'

Rufus was too busy getting out of that to think about what she'd just said. He concocted some wildly improbable tale about being in at Wanaka last week seeing a friend of his who owned motels and meeting three ministers' daughters, travelling together.

Marilla helped him out by sending the children off for bacon and eggs, which would make a quick lunch, and to see if any walnut crisps were left.

Rufus looked at her and grinned. 'I'll have to watch. I don't want any controversy with the kids over that. I'll tell Diana in my own good time. Imagine if they knew I'd put my spoke in and skittled the idea of that woman coming here. They'd come out with it the moment Di and Don got in the door ... *when* they do. And they'd think it was hilarious, their tough uncle being scared stiff of the husband-hunters.'

An edge crept into Marilla's tone. 'They're scarcely in the plural. One unusual woman doesn't make a – a whole pack of them, all after you, surely.'

Rufus blinked. Then, mildly, 'Sounded smug, did I? Sorry about that. As if I thought I was some sort of prize?'

'You did. And let me tell you, you're out of date. Really old-fashioned. It may have appeared the only career open to women back in Jane Austen's day, but it isn't now. It may surprise you, but women are quite emancipated. If we don't want to marry, we don't. It's not a question of being left on the shelf, we can marry if we wish to, *and* pursue our careers before and after marriage. Just because you've heard of one poor, misguided female who

81

longs to be married and live beyond the foothills, don't, imagine many women are so desperate they'd want to take a chance on someone they've not even seen!'

The reddish-brown eyes narrowed to laughing slits. 'You *do* get your dander up, don't you? You feel this Eleanor St. John has let the side down, and that I've got an outsize ego. Calm down. I know perfectly well that if this paragon of all the virtues had come up here she'd probably have hated the first sight of me. I'm no tall, dark, and handsome hero.' He shut up just as the children came back, arguing fiercely because there were just two caramel tarts left and which two were going to be lucky.

'Easily solved,' said Rufus, 'Marilla and I will have them. And less fighting – it slows things up. I want all hands outside after lunch. I want to examine all the culverts on Lantern Hill. Some may be blocked and you know the damage that can cause.'

They put the dishes in the washer with the others. Marilla said apologetically, 'I'm just going to throw the beds together. I hate the look of unmade beds. It's stupid, when we can't have unexpected visitors, but habits die hard.'

Jane thoughtfully crunched her uncle's leftover bacon rind . . . it was the best bit of all; she said, 'Mum always says there are compensations to everything, and at least when we are cut off by snow, we can spring-clean, or sweep the chimneys, without getting caught at it. Not a hope of visitors.'

'Famous last words!' Tony was to repeat with relish three hours later. Marilla left a huge pot of soup simmering on the back of the stove. It wasn't made to Cordon Bleu standards, there was no time to cool it, skim it, and add vegetables. It all had to go in at once, with some mutton bones she found in the fridge, but soup would be ideal when they came in, probably chilled to the bone if they were working in icy water. She siezed a huge enamel casserole and positively threw in an enormous number of carrots and a couple of tins of mixed vegetables and some onion salt for flavour. No time to do fresh veg. She scrubbed some potatoes, pricked them, put them around the outside of the casserole.

In this hill country every blocked culvert or water-course could spell danger and inconvenience. In one gulley they found some sheep marooned on an island that had formed overnight. It was in a wider gulley, but normally even lambs could leap the narrow stream that trickled down it.

Tony and Rufus studied it. It had blocked badly, with huge boulders and a couple of sizeable saplings that had been brought down had made a very effective dam. Rufus said, 'They'd be all right till the water goes down if we get no more rain tonight. But we can't depend upon it. I didn't like the sound of the forecast. If we get any more, this will become a torrent and the small island and the sheep will be swept away. I wish the men were here.'

Tony said, 'Wish we had some dynamite. Wouldn't it be beaut?'

'Daft thing, but I tell you what ... see how that tree trunk is wedged in and sticking up? If we could get a leverage on it and force it up, I reckon it'd dislodge that boulder and the whole lot would go.'

'Yes, I reckon it would. Perhaps we could all yank on it.'

'Too risky by far. Those other boulders might come down on top of us. We can't tell which way it might go. One bounce and we'd have a broken leg or worse to cope with. But go back to the implement shed and get that rope on the left side of the door – it's got an iron eye and hook attached. Know the one I mean? Good. We can get it round the trunk and it'll be long enough to reach that *ngaio* over there. We'll use that as a winding-post.'

While he was away they went on clearing smaller stuff that might serve to keep the bigger boulders wedged. Every little rush thus freed washed more away. Rufus worked them hard but he took no risks with them. The water was icy, though the sun was so hot on their backs they discarded their windcheaters.

Tony got back with the rope. Rufus evidently knew

what he was about. Nothing haphazard about this. It was like seeing a dam give way when suddenly the trunk levered up the largest boulder, and by putting every ounce of their strength into it, it toppled over and the force of the released water carried the others downhill. A quarter of an hour later the water this side of the island was a mere trickle, though it still flowed strongly on the other side. Rufus and Tony splashed across and, one each side, drove the sheep to leap through the shallow water remaining and gain the freedom of the hillside.

They'd dropped their haversack of flasks and sandwiches beside a huge fallen tree, bleached to whiteness through generations of years, and now they sat on it, munched their sandwiches, drank scalding coffee. Rufus looked sideways at Marilla; her eyes were raking the whole scene . . . the hillsides beyond and above the homestead were clothed with almost impenetrable bush; the rock faces between them glinted silver with streaming water, and though clouds amassed and dispersed continually about the peaks, the sky above was cerulean blue.

Up high like this, they were even above the lantern tower and were facing the cleft that looked directly out to Aspiring. It was a mountain of dreams, clothed in remote splendour, the knife-edge of its long Coxcomb Ridge leading to its summit, outlined as if in silver paint, its horned peak flinging a challenge across the lesser heights below.

Marilla was sure Elfreda had lost her heart here, to the mountains and to someone who had lived here. She wondered if Rufus might have had an uncle who had worked on the run. How sad it must have been to come here, to glimpse a dream world, and to have to turn one's back upon it. A lesson to *you*, Marilla, not to lose your heart to it.

She brought her gaze back and encountered Rufus's. 'You're enjoying every moment of this,' he accused her.

She looked shamefaced. 'I know it's been a catastrophe, that it's going to mean a long disruption to access and getting stock in and out, but – it's—' she waved a hand as if to emphasize that no words could do justice to such a scene.

Surprisingly, he didn't cut her down to city size. He said, 'I know. Sometimes we detest the elements, we groan and moan and wonder why our forebears ever took this land, but there isn't one of us could bear to live anywhere else.'

They left the tuckerbag beside the tree, worked off to the right, and into another gulley. It was easier work here.

Jane said, 'I'm starving again. I keep thinking of that soup and the casserole you said you put in. I hope you did a big one, Marilla, you mightn't be used to mountain appetites.'

Marilla laughed. 'I threw in every chop that was there; thought it could be re-heated another day if we were still busy outside.'

Two minutes later they were all standing stock-still and listening, amazed, their faces upturned in the direction of the hilltop. They were hearing voices. But how could they? Even if it had been Rufus's men returning, they wouldn't have come from the east.

The next moment they saw four figures come round the track just below the top. Four tired, almost exhausted figures. But they raised a shout of triumph as they saw the cluster of people below and the farm buildings. As they said later, it was the sweetest sight they'd ever seen.

With one accord the lower party downed their shovels and started up the hill. There were two fairly boyish figures, men in their early twenties, probably, one more mature, possibly in his thirties, and a tall, spare man who would be older. They had light packs on their backs, were certainly dressed for tramping, and well booted, but they looked as if their legs could cave in under them any time.

Rufus was surmising as they climbed towards them. 'We never get climbers from that direction. They don't appear sodden. Yet they must have crossed the Waihemo. Good heavens, they aren't survivors from a helicopter crash, I hope. There could have been one out looking for

85

someone lost. I ought to have stayed inside long enough to hear the news. Well, we'll soon know.'

They had to work their way round, and at times stands of trees or outcrops of rocks hid them from each other's view, but the sheep-tracks led them on towards a meeting.

The five from the homestead stopped on a grassy basin above a row of crags and let the others stumble down the last stretch towards them, as there was room here for all to stand almost level.

As they neared, Marilla became rooted to the spot with shock. The second one was her brother – well, half-brother – Guy! Good grief, here was a moment fraught with all sorts of possibilities. It was a moment of acute relief for these men bushed here among inhospitable mountains, cold, damp, exhausted, hungry. And she was about to be revealed as an impostor.

It took Guy a few seconds longer to realize he was indeed gazing at his sister. For one moment he'd thought he was going mad, next that it must be her double – for surely these two redheads were related? Then the expression on her face told him it was indeed Marilla. He cried her name aloud.

She had a flash of inspiration, born of her desperation. She ran forward crying, 'Guy ... and I thought you still in Britain!' and cast herself into his arms, lifting her face to be kissed as she hugged him. As he bent his bewildered face to do it, she hissed at him in a whisper, 'Don't let on who I am. They think my name is Sinjin. Leave it that way.'

He kept his arm round her, hugging her, saying, 'What on earth are you up to now?' then louder, for the benefit of the others, though they were not taking much notice but were exchanging greetings and explanations, 'I was told you were on holiday at Wanaka. I had the chance of coming home more quickly than I thought and decided to surprise M – my mother and father. Just walked in on them. I told them not to let you know, as I was to accompany the Head of my Department down on this Conservation Survey. I was sure I'd run into you somewhere.

If not, as we were going further south too, I was going to ring your parents before leaving here and find out where you were going next.'

Marilla turned to Rufus, said, 'This is a friend of mine from Wellington – who's been in Britain three years. Guy Stewart. But how did you all get here?'

The tall spare man was spokesman. 'I knew this area long ago. In fact, I once worked here. Remember me, Rufus? Though you were just a kid.' He swept on, not waiting for an answer. 'I took them up Goldpan Gully behind Fergusson's. We left the car at their homestead. We went up to their hut above the waterfalls. Then the storm hit. I wasn't a bit worried, thought we might have slippery hillsides to contend with, no more. But during that storm a bit of the hillside got torn away, leaving nothing but sheer bluffs. It would have been foolhardy to attempt the descent. I was confident we could go round the other side of it, but when we got there, we found a river where no river ever existed before. I still haven't got my bearings. It would go into the Motatapu, I'm sure. Our only hope was to make for here. I knew it would take us 'till nightfall, because we'd have to skirt round the Wai-hemo till we got to that small swing bridge away past, then cut back on the private road, but – look, tell me, am I going mad, or have you folk diverted the Waihemo, but how could you? Because when we reached the dividing point,' he swung round and gestured, 'we found the river-bed practically dry. We walked through.'

Rufus said, 'It happened during last night. The disappearing river of the legend suddenly disappeared, causing more disaster – it's joined the Blue and washed out our road.' His eyes suddenly narrowed. 'I've got it . . . you're Steve Ranaldson. But you were so much younger.'

The man laughed. 'So were you. About the size of this one.' He looked at Tony, said, 'Is he your son, Rufe?'

'No, my nephew. Di's son. It's good to see you. Blessing you knew this territory.'

'Aye. This is Lindsay McDiarmid and Boyd Fellowes, my assistants. They've stood up to it better than Guy and myself. We've been out of New Zealand a bit too long, though we did a fair bit of tramping in the Lake District and the Highlands. Our work took us there. I reckon my joints will creak like rusty hinges tonight. Man, am I glad to see the marks of civilization!'

Guy clapped the older man affectionately on the shoulder. 'Listen to him – he's still pretty tough. But boy, will hot baths go down well?'

They wasted no time. The visitors were pretty whacked by the time they reached the haven and warmth of the big kitchen. Marilla said, 'Before anything else, you must have some hot soup. I'll ladle it out right away. No style, just get at it.'

She was still avoiding Guy's puzzled looks. She wished he'd stop casting them at her. She hoped Steve Ranaldson didn't know he had a sister called Marilla.

Rufus picked up the phone, listened, they were still in touch. 'I'll let them know in Wanaka that you're here, and at Fergusson's too, or they'll have search parties out. Then I'll have some soup too.'

The talk was all of the storm, its consequences, its possible effects on the valleys, the strange fact that Stephen Ranaldson had worked here long ago.

They fell on the soup and bread with famished joy. Jane giggled, watching them, and said to Marilla in an aside, 'If they keep up eating like this, there'll be nothing left of your casserole. We'd better do an enormous mound of potatoes and I think we should take some of Mum's frozen apple pies out of the freezer, you can bake them from scratch. No time to thaw first.'

Marilla was terrified to leave Guy with Rufus, so she sent Jane to get them, and Tony for the potatoes. Then when it didn't seem too obvious, she said, 'I came up here exploring. I wanted to see all the valleys round here and my car broke down, so I stayed last night. But at least I can be of some use. The children's mother is in Auckland where her husband is in hospital, so Rufus Sinclair and the children were on their own. The men are up at the top hut. Quite an adventure, isn't it?'

Guy's eyes narrowed. 'You've been having a quite a few adventures lately, from what your mother told me. Time I was back to take care of you . . . it looks to me like a case of when the cat's away, the mice have a helluva time.'

Oh dear, when Guy was in a mood like this, he could easily go too far. He loved pretending things and would regard it all as a whale of a joke.

She tried to make light of it. 'Well, you couldn't expect me to stop the clock while you were in the Northern Hemisphere. I had to while away the time. Then after being away from teaching while Granny was ill, I thought I'd take a good long holiday before the next teaching year takes up.'

'I trust you intended coming back before my given date of arrival? I know I'm five weeks ahead of schedule, but a long holiday sounds very indefinite! Imagine me, flying in early to give everyone a surprise, and you not there! I had so much to tell and show you. Can't do justice to all that scenery by letter. I've some super slides.'

Marilla giggled. 'Surprises don't pay off every time. I'm not clairvoyant, you know.' Guy certainly sounded more a disappointed lover than a brother. She caught a look passing between Jane and Anne, a purely feminine and speculative look. She knew what they were thinking. Then Jane scowled. But why?

Each floor had a bathroom and separate showerbox, so no one had to wait. The four men returned to the kitchen and flopped.

'Many's the meal I've had here in the old days,' said Stephen Ranaldson, looking around with affection. 'That's what started me off on my interest in conservation. I owe so much to your father and grandfather, Rufus. They had the sensible approach . . . they wanted to preserve as much natural beauty for posterity as possible but were commonsense enough to know some sacrifices must be made to provide power for industry and the comforts of home life. Not that it was such an issue then, as now, but my first lesson in that attitude came when, though they were entitled to keep Blue Canyon to

89

themselves, they allowed access for tramping clubs over their own private roads leading to the hinterland.

'It fired my imagination. I went off to Scotland soon after I left here, and studied the whole thing at first hand. Jove, never when I was here did I imagine I'd be attached to the Ministry in an advisory capacity. I was just a rouse-about.'

Marilla liked him immensely, his whipcord spareness, the laughter crinkles at his eyes, the faint Scots burr acquired in those years, and his humility. No matter how high a position this man held, he wouldn't cover up his humble origin.

She grinned at him. 'But then you can't keep a Macdonell down, can you? And it's probably the Keppoch branch at that?'

He looked immensely surprised. 'Yes, it is, but what do you mean?'

'Just that they're descended from the Lord of the Isles.'

He said, looking at her with respect, 'How many people, especially of your age, would know the Ranaldsons belong to the Macdonell clan?'

She laughed. 'Not many. It's just that my mother is a Macdonell, but of Glengarry.'

'Och, aye. That branch emigrated to New Zealand in great numbers when the sixteenth chief sold the estates. I did a fair bit o' looking up when I was there. Guy joined me in a survey I was doing on the results of, and side-effects of, these big power projects in the Highlands. His mother was a Macdonell too, as of course, no doubt, you'd know.'

It was a tricky moment, but Guy said easily, 'That's how our families first met. Because they both had Macdonell ancestry. A clan reunion in New Zealand. They found they were practically neighbours back in the town they lived in. They met just before Marilla was born. I remember her well in her pram, with a dummy.'

A vigorous protest was wrung from Marilla. 'Guy! A dummy! My mother never in her life gave a baby a dummy. Why, even in those days they were considered unhygienic! You're making it up.'

The children giggled and Rufus said, chuckling, 'You were probably sucking a rusk, Marilla. Not to worry, it may not sound glamorous, but we were all babies once.'

Guy's voice was drawling. 'She certainly was no glamour-chick *then*. To look at her now, a red-haired beauty like Mary, Queen of Scots, you'd never dream what an ugly little ginger kid she was—'

'It's a great drawback knowing anyone from infancy,' cut in Marilla. 'You weren't exactly an Adonis yourself. I never remember you without lumps of skin off your nose and knees.'

But he was decidedly handsome now. Marilla was the image of her father, so no likeness to Guy could give her away. Guy was like their mother, black-haired, brown-eyed, with an angular severity of features for the masculine difference, that gave him quite a presence, a face that broke up easily into laughter, despite that severity in repose. Marilla thought Rufus was taking stock of him in a reflective sort of way.

The sun dropped behind the mountains in the sudden way it had here, and it was night. Marilla felt unreal . . . here she was, marooned in a homestead, with the brother she'd thought still in London, pretending to be someone else . . . at least *she* was pretending to be someone else. She must try to get Guy on his own tonight.

Concealing one's identity for an overnight stay was one thing, to keep it up with a relative near was another. And the situation was complicated enough without her attempting to explain now, with a houseful of guests. It could create tension. How awful . . . like being cooped up on a desert island with uncongenial companions. There was Guy's career to think of too; after all, this nice Stephen Ranaldson was his chief. It all sounded so stupid.

It wasn't fair to Rufus Sinclair to burden him with it. He was stuck here with three children to look after, a crowded household, and the possibility of being without power if further undermining took place. And he wasn't even flapping. She had to admire him. He'd been brought up to battle with the elements and to accept what he couldn't change. A basic acceptance like that stood one in good stead. The stillness at the heart of the storm such as Dad had preached on just last month.

CHAPTER SIX

STEPHEN RANALDSON was in great form reliving the past. They suspected he was even grateful to the storm for marooning him.

'You'd have called in here, of course?' asked Rufus.

'Sure. After we'd had a good look over the Track from Fergussons', then the stretch from their hut across the Waihemo Terrace, we were going back to their place, to pick up the car and come in here by the Canyon Road. I'd hoped, of course, to see Sholto and Isobel.'

'They'll be horribly disappointed, Steve. I remember them saying, among other things they hoped to do, that they were going to see if they could trace you. They knew the sort of work you were engaged in when you first went over. They'd had a card from you in your first few months over there. They decided you'd be married and settled down long ago. Are you? Married, I mean?'

'No, still a bachelor, more's the pity.' Stephen made a quaint little suggestion of a bow towards Marilla, serving the coffee. 'I'm one of the unlucky ones, Miss Sinjin.'

She smiled, not without malice. 'How refreshing to find someone who considers it unlucky. Rufus here still has the quaint idea that women are husband-hunters.'

She saw Guy look at her curiously and averted her gaze quickly.

Guy drawled, 'If you were here long enough, and that road was open, he'd be convinced it was the other way round. Your mother said she was fair tired of your boy-friends. And so, it seemed, were you. Not to worry, now I'm back I'll keep them all at bay.'

Oh dear, if only he knew the situation here. She must get him alone and tell him the whole thing – otherwise he'd say something outrageous and spill the beans. She said severely, 'You make me sound a *femme fatale*. I get very tired of all this talk about marriage. It's not the only career. I've a few things I'm far more interested in.'

Rufus had a sarcastic drawl in his voice. 'It seems extraordinary when you're so domesticated.'

Marilla could have choked them both. 'I'm very fond of home life, my parents' home in particular, but for me it doesn't have to be centred round a husband. Tell me, Mr. Ranaldson, did you find connections in Scotland, and see places connected with the clan history?'

'Aye, that I did. Magnificent country, not far from Fort William mostly, and with yours the other side of Loch Lochy, Miss Sinjin.'

'Oh, do call me Marilla. Cooped up like this, I don't feel we can stand on ceremony.'

'I'd like that fine. Marilla ... my word, that's a great name for here. Have they shown you all the Green Gables place names yet?'

'No, they've not had time. But I believe there's a Rainbow Valley.'

'Yes, and it's the abode of rainbows to make it even more authentic.' He turned to Rufus. 'Do you still have a string of bells hung in the big aspen there, to make it just like Montgomery's Rainbow Valley?'

Rufus nodded. 'But not the same string. They rust out at times, but we always replace them. You won't find much changed.'

'Good. Man, I'd like fine to be out with you on the hill tomorrow. How about it? I reckon there'll be enough work from this storm for an extra hand or two to be welcome?'

'We'll use you all. Let's get the dishes done now – we've got the washer loaded with the entire day's crocks. We should all be sitting round for the seven o'clock news. There'll be pictures of the flooding and of the broken ridges – they'd get through so far for those. I didn't hear any helicopter, though. So we wouldn't get pictures of beyond the Motatapu.'

Personal problems receded as they watched pictures of the disaster areas on the screen. Stephen and his men were mentioned as having been reported safe at Blue

Canyon Homestead. Almost all the Matukituki Valley had been flooded with the immense volume of water from the diverted Waihemo pouring into it, in addition to its own share of the cloudburst.

The West Wanaka Station was isolated except for lake access which would be used in an emergency.

'That was where the Queen Mother did some fishing once,' said Jane, with relish. 'Wouldn't it have been marvellous to have this happen then, and be isolated with a member of the Royal Family?'

'With the Royal Princes,' said Anne, eyes astar, 'what a story that'd make!' Like a shadow she disappeared to get a scribbling pad, then returned to her stool.

'Oh, gosh,' said Tony, 'look at her . . . she'll be writing a story about it. With herself as heroine no doubt, and one of the Princes falling for her. Who do you fancy, Anne, Andrew or Edward? What nuts girls are!'

Fortunately Anne wasn't in the least self-conscious. She stuck her small nose in the air. '*You* are not a writer, Tony. You have no imagination. And in any case,' witheringly, 'I'm not so stupid as to see myself on the Throne of England. I'll have my Johanna, a girl my age, stage-manage a romance with someone at a station like ours, and royalty. But which one of the Royals?'

Her uncle was convulsed. 'Anne, I think you'd better leave the Royal Family out of your stories. Too complicated by far. You could use this situation, of course. Steve, what a pity you haven't been knighted. Sir Stephen would sound almost as good as a prince.'

'Not really,' objected Anne, 'You can't use the term "Your Royal Highness" to a mere knight. Besides, Mr. Ranaldson's too old for a hero!'

Stephen was chuckling. 'I quite realize forty-five is out of the question, but how about Vice-Royalty, Anne? A Governor-General. I think "Your Excellency" would sound pretty good. Oh dear, *they* don't come very young, either, the Guvs. I know, he could have a really dashing *aide-de-camp* accompanying him. He could be a viscount or the heir to a dukedom – even a young duke himself.'

Anne was enraptured and scratched away madly. 'What do you call viscounts or dukes? Oh, I bet nobody knows.'

Stephen said, 'A viscount would be called "My Lord" and addressed as "Your Lordship". The Duke would be "My Lord Duke" and addressed as "Your Grace". Though—' he stopped short.

Tony prompted him, 'Though you don't really think we've ever had viscounts and dukes as *aides*, do you?'

'Well, no,' admitted Stephen cautiously, 'but there's always a first time. Mind you, Anne, you'd probably only be able to use those terms at first, because if he got marooned here, they'd probably be calling him Bill or Jake the first time he helped them with the crutching.'

'Well, that wouldn't matter, long's I got plenty of the other terms in first. We can use Marilla as the heroine, stranded here exactly as she was. Then bang, they come together with it all – what's the word? You know, the children do it?'

'Engineered. With it all engineered by Johanna and her brother and sister. In other words, by Anne, Tony, and Jane.'

Tony, alarmed, said, 'Hey, leave me out of it!'

Marilla said hastily, 'Me too. That viscount sounds young. I'm nearly twenty-eight.'

Rufus was surprised. 'Not really? Good heavens, I thought you were much younger.'

She pulled a face. 'You ought to hear me in the classroom! I sound like an aged dragon. Anne, I don't think it would do apart from age. If he's blue-blooded his people would oppose him marrying me. I'm too plebeian.'

Anne said spiritedly, 'That's not a stumbling block, Marilla. You'd be travelling under an assumed name too. You were brought up in a Scottish castle, and your people are so wealthy, you've come out to New Zealand to be loved for yourself alone. When you realize the duke wants to marry you whoever you are, you know that it's truly love. Then you tell him your real name.'

Tony said, 'Well, you'd better not call her Sinjin.

Honest Injun, if she was travelling incognito she'd be Smith or Jones.'

Guy's eyes met Marilla's, and looked away.

Anne said, 'There, I've done my jotting. It's well known that all writers should do their jotting as soon as they get their inspiration. I'll write that tomorrow morning.'

Her uncle lowered his tawny brows. 'You'll be in the schoolroom tomorrow morning, enough time's been lost. I've got four extra men now. I'll set you your work, and perhaps Marilla would look in from time to time. This is the last term and you've got no show of catching up if you miss much now. I'll put you on your honour to be good. Marilla won't have much time.' He turned to Marilla. 'I'll help you all I can, we all will. But no frills. Cook everything the easiest way and serve it without style. One thing, I won't need to do any killing. We'd better use all we can out of the deep freeze. I've no faith in the power lines holding.'

Stephen scooped Anne off her stool to sit on his knee. 'Keep at your writing, little one. Don't let anyone tease you out of it. Every writer's got to start at the bottom. Not like a family business that can be handed on. And jotting down immediately is a must, like you said.'

Anne beamed on him. Children loved grown-ups who took them seriously. 'Nanny told me I must do that. They had a girl here once who was a writer, you see. She could draw too and always took sketches of every animal, leaf, bird, tree. And lots of other things. But Jane does *my* drawings. So does Tony when I can get him to. They're both wizards at it. This girl became a well-known writer. We have all her books.'

Marilla knew it. Long before Stephen asked the inevitable, 'Who?'

'Frederica Moorcroft.'

Jane said quickly, 'I'll get some. They're just here. You'll recognize some of the places.' She brought them over. Three faces bent over them.

Frederica was formed from Elfreda, of course, and Moorcroft was her middle name. Elfreda had been so shy, so scared of the aunts not approving when first she began to write, she had done it all anonymously, having her mail sent to the office where she was a typist. Later, when Aunt Myrtle had praised one of the books after a good review had appeared in a literary journal, she'd plucked up courage to tell.

As Marilla leaned over to look too, she realized now why Rufus's profile had seemed so familiar. Not only were all these sketches of Blue Canyon, as she'd recognized almost immediately, but the redheaded children of the series were based on Rufus and Diana and Kathleen. Though they had other names. Elfreda had never, even to Marilla, breathed the source of her inspiration.

She looked up and noticed Rufus was looking at Stephen as if he was impatient for him to comment. Did Rufus know who Fredrica Moorcroft was, then? Of course, he must. Wow! Was he waiting for Stephen to click? But would he remember one girl out of all the students who had worked here in their vacations?

Stephen was saying, 'How well they're done. Here's the donkey house and old Brumby's quarters. I think that's gone now.' He went on leafing over and came to the back cover, the inside of it. Frederica Moorcroft always had tricky little sketches on the inside covers. This one showed a weeping willow, trailing its fingers in a stream. Beside it was a gnarled old *ngaio* with a rustic bench of rough-barked wood under it. The legend beneath said: *The Place of Dreams-come-true.* Jane put a small forefinger on it. 'That was where the children found an old tin cash-box buried. That proved Rainbow Homestead – as she called it – did legally belong to their father and mother. Even if pots of gold weren't always found at the foot of rainbows. I wish *we'd* known Frederica.'

Stephen said slowly, 'I did, of course. That was the last summer I was here. I didn't know she'd ever made it – publication, I mean. She was very shy about her gifts, and gifts they undoubtedly were. That wasn't her real name, of course.'

'No, it was Elfreda Grant. Mum told us. Nanny was

98

having a tough time, everything breaking down. The plant, the kerosene fridge, the lot. Someone in Wanaka brought this girl out and she offered to help. Oh dear,' Jane looked aghast. 'Mum said she was shy too, and didn't want anyone to know her real name. Mum wrote her through the publishers, when she first discovered the books. But no one here would tell anyone, would they?'

Stephen ruffled her hair. She was leaning against him on the couch. 'Well, I knew it already, so not to worry. She may not care now anyway.'

A voice behind Marilla spoke, Guy's. 'She doesn't care now. I know her well. She had two holy terrors of aunts who brought her up. She didn't let them know till she was established.'

Stephen Ranaldson looked startled. 'And you've never said?'

Guy looked startled too. 'Why should I? Children's books never cropped up in any of our conversations, Steve.'

Stephen said, 'No, of course not.' His eyes dropped to another page, the dedication one. 'To Kit and Fiona', he read. 'Her own children, I suppose?'

Guy said, 'Oh, no, she never married. I can't think why. She still looks after those aunts. My mother knows them well.'

Marilla was only thankful that she and Guy had been too old to have children's books dedicated to them when Elfreda's success came. She supposed Guy couldn't resist claiming he knew her.

She thought she'd better endorse what had been said, otherwise Guy might give her away. 'I know her too. I thought the places looked familiar, but we've been too busy to think about it much.'

Rufus said, 'Now, as soon as the News Brief comes on, you children must be off to bed. Marilla can come across to the Lantern Tower with me. I must signal the men. She did very well last night. I must make quite sure they're okay. I mean, she did well this *morning* – it was just before daybreak. It seems incredible that it's not twenty-four hours away yet.'

Marilla was still in her Macdonell of Glengarry tartan trews, with a bright green bulky sweater pulled over them, glad now of her mother's foresight. Rufus Sinclair took a three-quarter coat off a hook on the back porch. It had belonged to Kathleen. Its hood was lined with the Sinclair tartan. He held it for her. She said, 'I'll put it on myself. You might jerk your thumb.'

'It's much better. Come on.' She slipped into it. He smiled, 'But you'll have to tie it under your chin yourself.'

He caught her elbow as they crossed a little humpy-backed bridge over the creek, and brought her to a stop. 'Wait, I want to listen.'

They stood very still and close, holding their breath. Here was a man who knew the sounds of his own world so well, he could detect differences.

Then he said, 'That river is still running much more heavily than I expected by now. I thought only part of its waters might have been diverted. I don't think any of us can estimate the damage or the length of time we'll be cut off. How will that affect you, Marilla?'

She was a little puzzled. 'I've already said it doesn't matter much. I'm not in a job at the moment. I won't fret. I won't feel cooped up.'

She sensed rather than saw that he wasn't entirely satisfied. In the moonlight his face seemed all planes and angles. Then he said, 'Perhaps having Stewart here has made it more endurable for you?'

'I'm glad he's here, yes. The more company the better in a time like this. They can all help. He's not just a white-collar wallah. He spent some of his Varsity vacations on high-country farms, once on Lilybank, up Tekapo, which is even more isolated than this. There's no road right through. It ends at the river which they have to cross by four-wheel drive trucks. He's no city slicker.'

The hand on her elbow tightened impatiently. 'I wasn't criticizing Guy. I realized from their talk of their work in the Highlands that he'd be a good chap to have round. I was wondering how you'd have stuck it out if someone you knew so well hadn't arrived.'

'I can't see it matters. Lovely to see him, of course, after three years, but as far as the company's concerned, to me it just means four more men to cook for. That's an awful lot of extra potatoes and carrots to peel, a lot more cookies to disappear as fast as you can make them.'

He laughed. 'I reckon you're the sort to cope. Anyway, there are tins and tins of factory biscuits in the store-room.' Something struck him. 'Three years ... that's a hell of a time.'

She frowned, looking up. 'What do you mean? Why, Steve Ranaldson's been away twenty. Lots of chaps stay in Britain longer than that.'

She saw his mouth twitch. 'You seem to be singularly lacking in vanity. What else could I mean but that it was a long time to be away from a girl like you? I wouldn't have taken the risk.'

She got such a shock, she stepped back from him a little. His hands shot out and clutched her and he winced involuntarily. She said, 'Watch that thumb. You must take no chances with it.'

'I can't take chances with you either. No rails on this bridge. The creek's not deep, but the water's icy. Imagine if you got a chill and I had to cope with this lot on my own.'

'You'd do very well – you seem very self-sufficient to me.'

'Do I? But that's just my brave front.' The slightly lazy drawl that was natural to him made him sound cynical at times.

Marilla shrugged beneath his hands, aware crossly that she was oddly conscious of them. 'I hardly think so. Not the way you were prepared to bolt when someone who sounded ideal for a high-country wife was prepared to come here.'

His voice held scorn. 'Oh, the estimable Eleanor St. John – good heavens! Yes, I'd run a mile from that one. Marilla, you're changing the subject. I said I'd not have risked leaving you for three years.'

'What am I supposed to reply to that? How could it matter?'

'Can't you guess how it matters to me? I'll cross the t's and dot the i's. I want to know if Guy Stewart has any particular claim on you. I like these things clearly defined.'

Marilla made herself sound cross because she was struggling with some hitherto unknown emotions. 'I think you're mad. But I'll answer you, though it's hardly your business. Guy and I have been fond of each other for years, but more like brother and sister than anything else.' There!

'Is that true?'

'Any reason why it shouldn't be true?'

'Yes, the way he looked at you tonight.'

'Oh, bosh. Result of three years away.'

'And you?'

'Me?'

'How did you feel ... meeting him again after all that time. And how had you felt when he went away?'

'When he went away? Mr. Sinclair, don't you think this is a—'

'Yes, it's a cheek. But don't go back to Sinclair. It's plain ridiculous away up here. All right, I'll let it go.'

'I think you'd better,' she said shortly, and when he immediately walked on, knew it was absurd to feel it was something of an anti-climax.

They came to the stable and Rufus put out a hand for the switch by the door. Nothing happened. 'Blast! The bulb must have gone. You'd better let me guide you, I know every step.' His arm was warm about her. He counted as they ascended the very narrow wooden stairway. 'There are twenty-three, but you'll see the top one by the light of the tower. I know it takes a funny turn, this stair, but you can see a glimmer. I've got you.'

As soon as they reached the second of top stair she freed herself.

They made their signals, the men had heard the news, knew by it that they had guests, and they could expect them tomorrow afternoon.

Rufus seemed in no hurry. He went across to an immense hurricane lamp, checked it was full of kerosene. 'I want it really in case the power goes. The tower light shines into my room. I always wake if it goes out.'

'But surely no one will be in need of it. The access is cut, the bridges are down. No one will come.'

'It's a tradition to have it always alight. Once in a while a crazy loon attempts a climb without telling anyone. Mind, he'd have had to be up here two days ago to be lost now, but we take no chances. In my grandfather's time three men would have lost their lives but for that light. They just made it. They did each lose some of their toes with frostbite. We take no risks.'

Marilla said softly, 'I think it's wonderful to know it's been burning day and night, through all the years, on the remote chance of saving someone who, in direct contrast, cares nothing about other people.'

They exchanged a look, an odd look. There was nothing much in what she'd just said, yet it seemed to her as if a rapport had been established. She dropped her eyes.

He hesitated, then said, 'I'll show you something that may make you feel we still have contact with the rest of the world. Come over here.'

There was a small set of sturdy steps like library steps, under the window that looked out towards the cleft that gave that tiny view of the lake. There was just room for them to stand. He shuffled till his shoulders cut out the bright light behind them. He had to put his left arm round her shoulders to steady her.

'Look straight ahead into that darkness. You can, in daytime, see the far shore. Not this shore, of course. Now slightly to the right, you ought to get it. It only looks as big as a star. It's the homestead lantern of an over-lake property. Got it?'

Yes, she'd got it. He said, 'That lake is a route of commerce in a small way, a link with civilization. Sometimes I think that because we get so small a glimpse of it, we

103

prize it more.'

She said, moved, 'It's so still tonight, the west wind is indeed sleeping on the lake. Thank you, Rufus.' He helped her down.

They came to the stairway. 'Now let me take you. Going down is even more tricky, in the dark. I'll go slightly ahead.' He held up his good hand to her, gripping her waist with it. 'Lean on my shoulder, then if you slip, you can't go far.'

He didn't count aloud going down, so she thought presently that she was on the last step and found her foot going into space instead. She flung out a hand to steady herself, pitched forward, and Rufus received her into his arms as she fell.

Her 'Whoops!' was drowned out by his chuckle. Now why chuckle?

'Why are you laughing?' she demanded.

'Don't be so naïve ... that was precisely what I was hoping for ... here goes!'

She was held against him, began a protest, and was very effectively silenced. She tried to push him away, but she found his shoulder as unyielding as Stalwart Crag above Lantern Hill.

She closed her eyes against the feelings that surged through her, feelings she didn't want to recognize ... delight, enchantment even. This, then, was what kissing was supposed to be. Till now she'd thought it vastly overrated. Greater depths underlay this: a sort of fundamental magnetism, swamped by a desire to give and keep giving and to receive. At that moment he lifted his mouth from hers.

'No doubt I ought to apologize. But it was irresistible. I hope you found it as enjoyable as I did.'

The sheer effrontery of his light tone gave her time to recover from the surprising intensity of her feelings. She drew in a deep breath she sorely needed and said tartly, 'Well, all I can say, Mr. Sinclair, is this: if you're as susceptible as this to close quarters with a girl, if your sister and mother had succeeded in getting the husband-hunting Eleanor up here, you'd probably have found yourself wedded to her before Christmas!'

He burst out laughing. 'My dear Miss Sinjin, did anyone ever tell you what a waspish tongue you have? Suits me all right, though – I do enjoy a verbal battle. Now this Eleanor, she'd probably have sickened me by agreeing with everything I said, cooed and simpered.'

Marilla gave way to real mirth. When she sobered up she said, 'It might be interesting to meet her. She might be all you'd want in a wife.'

'I know exactly what I want in a wife.'

'Then I think it's hardly likely you'll ever get married. It's a very bad thing to have such definite ideas.'

She stepped outside. He came after her, caught her fingers to hold her back, said 'Ouch!' having used his right hand.

She said, callously, 'Now if I was really waspish, I'd mutter "Serve you right." But I won't. I have a very forgiving nature.'

He only chuckled. He came to her other side, took that arm. 'Now, don't flee. I promise not to kiss you again ... tonight. I don't want you falling over and doing yourself an injury. We're going to depend upon you very much the next week or two. And I was only going to keep you here till I asked you something, not attempt another kiss.'

'Ask me what?'

'If *you* had definite ideas. About a husband?'

'No, what made you think I might have?'

'I thought that might account for your not being snapped up before.'

She laughed; she must keep it light. 'Perhaps it's a case of: "nobody asked me, sir, she said." '

'I can't believe that, it isn't true, is it?'

Laughter bubbled up in Marilla, as she thought of those last few weeks. Somehow this was putting it in its right perspective. It had seemed like sheer persecution at the time.

'No, it's not true. But thanks for the compliment.'

'Why didn't you accept any of them?'

She didn't answer. He repeated his question. She said, 'Don't you realize, Rufus, strangers don't ask such intimate questions. You can't expect me to confide all the secrets of my life to you, surely, when the day before yesterday I didn't even know such a person as Rufus Sinclair existed?'

'Time is a very debatable subject. Isn't that the unanswerable question? What *is* time?'

'As far as I'm concerned, this very moment, the only label I could put on time would be bedtime. Come on, I've had enough of this.'

He had all the persistence of a very young child. 'Why didn't you marry any of them? Was it because none of them roused a response in you?'

She wished he hadn't put it like that. She was well aware her response to him had been instinctive. She could only hope he'd not recognized it. She said, 'Don't take all Guy says so literally. He exaggerates and teases.'

'That's not an answer.' They had reached the cottage verandah. 'You're not going in without answering me, Marilla.'

She said slowly, 'Then I'm afraid you'll have to be content with this: I'm just not the marrying kind. Don't get any ideas about me, Rufus Sinclair. You lead a very womanless life up here. You seem far too susceptible. I mightn't be all you think I am. Just remember that, will you?' She opened the door, shed the coat, went through to the warmth and sanity of the kitchen.

Earlier she'd made up beds in the rooms of the cottage and the electric blankets had been on for ages to air the beds. Marilla began to grate the cheese for the toast and put out some chocolate chippie biscuits the girls had thawed from the deep freeze. They looked at the late news, and what they heard made them realize how fortunate they had been not to lose stock like the others.

Guy, Lindsay and Boyd washed and dried the supper dishes while Marilla set the table for the morning, sliced an enormous stack of bread for toast with the slicer, and felt glad she could call it a day even if she hadn't managed a private conversation with Guy. It would have to wait.

Only Rufus and Marilla were left in the kitchen. The phone rang. 'It will be Diana ringing from Auckland,' said Rufus, going to it. 'I expect she'd be at the hospital when the earlier news was on and has just heard.'

Poor Diana was aghast. She'd heard too about the four men who'd turned up safe and sound. How awful – all those extra men to cook for, and heaven only knew when access would be restored. The girls couldn't manage to cook for all that crowd. Would Buck help them? Could he be spared? He wasn't too bad on cooking . . .

Rufus cut in, 'We're okay, Di, let me explain. Talk about incredible luck. An answer to prayer dropped out of the skies. A Miss Sinjin. She can cook, is experienced in first-aid and a teacher to boot. She got stranded up here in her Mini. Engine conked out. At the time I blew my top, but she calmed me down. Now I'm wondering what we'd have done without her. She used to live at Fairlie so likes the mountains, is marvellous with the kids, and believe it or not, Sis, when I dislocated my thumb, she calmly shoved it back. Oh, yes, not the sort to swoon, our Miss Sinjin.'

Marilla stood there, aghast. Rufus took it for no more than dismay at being described as such a paragon. If only he'd known she was terrified at the thought that if he kept repeating her name, Diana might just tumble. Women were quicker than men in the matter of names. They were more interested in them. Marilla found she was gritting her teeth.

Diana must have sounded relieved. Rufus went on, 'I reckon she'd not turn a hair if the lot of us went down with measles – she helped us clear out all the culverts today, she'd make a wonderful governess for up here, what say I try to persuade Miss Sinjin to stay? She's not in a position right now. I gather she was nursing a relative. How about it, shall I give it a go?'

Marilla began madly shaking her head at him to indicate that she couldn't. Diana must have thought this

107

paragon was off to bed because she quite evidently made some teasing remark. Rufus roared.

'Smitten? Of course I'm smitten. An answer to prayer, I said. But not a matchmaker's prayer. You ought to see her. A heart of gold, but everyone's idea of a Victorian governess, no less. So much the better – you know what always happened to our governesses? They married the shepherds and moved nearer town. I reckon this one would stay for ever. I'll have a good bash at persuading her. Then I could let this Miss St. John know the position is filled.'

He went on to say, 'And guess who the V.I.P. is? You mightn't have recognized the name. None less than Steve Ranaldson – remember the hand we had who went off to Scotland? So much for Mum and Dad trying to contact him over there! Well, Sis, we're quite okay. I'll keep in touch as long as we don't get the phone cut off if another storm hits us. And whatever happens, don't let Donal get any ideas, when he's discharged, of even coming down to Wanaka. Once there, he'd probably get a helicopter to come through, and we want him within reach of a doctor in case of further complications. We get too many days of hazardous flying conditions. No, you can't speak to her, Di, she's fast asleep. Early to bed, early to rise, that's our Miss Sinjin. She's the same type as old Trudy who used to be at Belle Knowes. Keep your fingers crossed, old girl. If I play it right we could have her for keeps.'

As he hung up Marilla's legs could hold her no longer and she sank on to a chair. She put her head in her hands and groaned. 'What on earth possessed you to pitch a tale like that?'

He just didn't give a darn. He too sank on to a chair and gave way to mirth. 'Oh, my dear Miss Sinjin, if only you could see your face!'

She fixed him with a stern eye that could have done credit to her word-picture as painted to his sister by Rufus Sinclair. 'What a tarradiddle! And it's got no future.'

He pulled his face straight. 'You mean you won't consider staying? But it's too early to make up your mind.'

'I mean nothing of the kind – no, at least I – oh, you've got me all tied up. Of course I won't be staying, and if you knew more about me, you might be glad of that. I meant that if your sister gets home, by helicopter, before I leave, finding me instead of the fiftyish spinster described, she's going to be very suspicious of your motives. What were they, anyway?'

'Well, for one thing it served her right. For another, if I'd told her you were a ravishing redhead, she would imagine I was falling for you fast, and would probably ring Brigid Granville and rejoice! It would then be all over Wanaka. On the other hand, if she thought I was pretending you had all the womanly virtues, she'd think I'd fallen for this little bit of fluff they dread me marrying. And whether you stay or not, my dear Miss Sinjin, at least you've provided me with a watertight excuse for not engaging the man-eating Eleanor.'

'It would serve you right,' said Marilla, trying not to laugh, 'if in years to come, when you're a lonely old bachelor, in need of a helpmeet, you meet this Eleanor, happily married to some lucky man, and find her positively beautiful and charming. You may have passed up the chance of a lifetime.'

'I'll risk it,' said Rufus.

'And you're probably in for the very father and mother of a row when your sister and her husband get home and I take my leave.'

The reddish-brown eyes met hers squarely. 'Are you so sure you'll want to, when the time comes?'

Her grey eyes were cool, hostile. 'I can imagine I'll be a little sad to leave the mountains, just as one is always sad to leave the beauty of the tourist areas. That's all, so if you were meaning anything more—' she floundered.

'Anything more personal?' he prompted her. 'Yes, I was.' He burst out laughing and came to sit on the table, swinging his long legs. 'What a strange, intriguing mixture you are, Marilla – one moment hot in defence of the amorous Eleanor, the next down on marriage like a ton of bricks. Why? How contradictory – which is the real Marilla?'

'It isn't contradictory. It ties in with the same thing. I very much dislike the vain way you assume this Eleanor would find you the answer to her prayer, even if she would like a high-country husband. So your attitude doesn't make me any more in favour of marriage than I used to be. It's hardly the be-all and end-all of existence.'

This time she got a little under his skin. He showed the red of anger, said shortly, 'Pity we hadn't had this talk before I spoke to Di. I mightn't have called you a paragon. I'm afraid I've very little time for women who despise the marriage bond. It's the family unit, the base of our society. Whenever it's flouted, civilization comes crashing. I don't like the teachers of our children despising it.'

Marilla knew a satisfaction she was ashamed of later, saying her prayers. At the moment she knew a human satisfaction that she'd set back this man who'd thought of her – as Eleanor – as a husband-hunter. Now he was resenting the fact that *she* wasn't.

She smiled thinly. 'You've got yourself snarled up, Rufus Sinclair. I don't despise marriage. I love family life. I believe in it. All I said was that marriage certainly isn't in *my* scheme of things.'

He opened his mouth to reply, but the door from the cottage wing opened and in came Guy. He had on a fisherman-knit jersey with a big roll collar, and he dangled Marilla's anorak. 'Come on, I've been very patient. Let's have a dander outside. Three years is a long time. And there's a moon.'

Marilla hid a smile as she saw Rufus check himself. She was sure he'd been going to come all over Head-of-the-House and say it was too late. She went across to Guy and slid her arms into the jacket he held out.

Rufus couldn't help himself, evidently. He said, stiffly, 'Stewart, she's had a whale of a day and if my men get down tomorrow, she'll have a young army to cook for, to say nothing of supervising lessons.'

Guy's twinkle appeared, transforming his face. 'A wander in the moonlight is rejuvenating to most people. I guarantee to put the spring back in her step, the sparkle in her eye.'

'Out!' said Marilla, propelling him to the door. But as he stepped outside she darted back. Rufus was still staring after them, and looked, as she turned, as if he thought she'd changed her mind.

But all she said was: 'I nearly forgot. Would you mind taking some stuff out of the deep freeze for me so it'll defrost? A leg of mutton, and some chops, a string of sausages and a bag each of yams, beans, and peanut cookies.'

'Right.' He looked at her across his folded arms, perked his head towards the door. 'I take it, then, that though you don't fancy marriage, you've no objection to men's company?'

She managed not to laugh, said seriously, 'How right you are. I enjoy it. Good-night, Rufus.'

CHAPTER SEVEN

She caught up with Guy outside. They picked their way through the little sheltered garden to a tiny octagon-shaped summerhouse, trellised over with clematis and honeysuckle, and went inside.

Guy stretched out his long legs, said, 'And now, my dear Eleanor Marilla St. John, will you tell a poor bewildered brother what the hell this is all about?'

Marilla gave way to mirth. Then she sobered up. 'Oh, how thankful I am I can now see the funny side of it. Guy, you were magnificent! My word, three years in the hub of the universe has improved you no end. Oh, how I admired the way you caught on.' And she proceeded to tell him the whole story.

When she had finished, and they had both had a hearty laugh over it all, they wandered back. Guy was to sleep in the cottage. He opened the back door for her, said, 'Well, you to your chaste couch, I to my monastic cell.'

Guy had always talked like that. From an upstairs window a light was falling on his face. It seemed incredible her brother should be here, stalwart, fine, infinitely dear. She reached up and put her two hands round his face, stood on tiptoe, said, 'How truly lovely to have you back, not just in New Zealand, but here. Good-night, love,' and she kissed him.

Guy was moved, but laughed to hide it. 'Goodness, absence *does* make the heart grow fonder! Goodnight, Rilla.'

She heard movement above. The light went out, the window was pushed up. Well, if Rufus Sinclair had witnessed and heard that, all to the good. He wouldn't suspect her of any designs on him, even after that tender moment at the foot of the stairs.

The days were terrifically busy, cut off in their own small

world. It seemed so strange, phoning through their weather reports each morning, listening in to the New Zealand news and the BBC news, so that voices reached them from Wellington, from London, a link right round the world, yet never the sound of a car apart from the homestead vehicles, because of the gap in that road, torn through by that volume of water.

Diana rang a couple of times, but always late, so Rufus made sure he answered the phone. Stephen rang his department, said this had been a most interesting development, and he'd stay on here to make reports and later, when conditions permitted, to go up to the huts above Blue Canyon as had been planned.

Every day they inspected the new outlet in a party. The river was settling, of course, from its earlier flooded conditions, but it changed daily. Stephen was an authority, Guy was second to him in knowledgeability, and the two younger men thought themselves incredibly fortunate to be on hand when this happened. Rufus and his three shepherds were mountain men and knew this terrain so well they could be almost called experts too. Marilla felt she absorbed geology and mountain-lore, hour by hour, like a piece of blotting paper.

It would pose some problems for the engineers restoring the bridge over the Matukituki, Stephen told them, to allow for greater volume of water permanently diverted into that river. Greater and longer approaches might have to be made. And that, of course, would take priority over this. Especially as there had never been a bridge here. They'd have to wait, too, to judge how much scouring-out would be likely to take place down in the sides of the Blue Canyon, above which the existing road, or what was left of it, hung. A lot of blasting would have to be carried out, and it was quite possible they would take the road into one of the gulleys, and build a bridge back in among the hills at a part much less likely to suffer from future erosion. A long, long job.

Marilla found a hand on her left and one on her right had slipped into hers. Two little voices spoke simultaneously, 'I'm glad *you're* here, Marilla.'

Rufus heard it, swung round, and his lips twitched. 'Not half as glad as I.' The tawny eyes met Marilla's grey ones. She was aware of a gladness she didn't want to feel. They were all looking at her, even Buck, Coll, Evan. What on earth was the matter with her? She was finding it hard to maintain a casual look. Then Rufus laughed. 'With a crowd like this to feed, even Buck might have got stage fright at the cooking.'

Marilla said, 'I hope you realize how much of the meal prep Buck does while I'm in the schoolroom. Those mounds of potatoes, carrots and onions he peels save my reason.'

Buck said, 'Yeah, but fair go, Marilla, you provide the variety. I'm limited. I just slash off some mutton, put in some fat and shove it in the oven with some veg and hope for the best. Even my gravy's temperamental. I'd never be able to slap up those curries and sauces. And your pastry is a dream.'

She laughed. 'You're doing things for my ego, but honesty forces me to admit I'm only doing the things I know I can do. My fruit cakes are lamentable. I'm always sure they're too soft, or too dry, and add, but never with judgement. And plenty of other things too. But Mum was a fair taskmaster. She even taught Guy to cook.' She stopped dismayed.

Guy came in quickly, 'You see, even when Marilla was quite small, I still had a thing about her. So I used to beat the eggs. I was besotted enough even to wash the dishes after her.'

Marilla rushed on, 'And when I was looking after Granny, and my sister and brother were out at lectures, I had a bit of time to experiment. I found, to my surprise, I quite enjoyed it, and as Dad keeps poultry, my mistakes didn't mean complete waste. Mind you, I don't think it always agreed with the chooks. Dad came back once to find they'd stopped laying. I didn't enlighten his mystification . . . the change of diet had put them off.'

Rufus said, 'When he came back once? I thought when

you said you were housekeeping for them they must have had an overseas trip.'

Marilla said quickly, 'No, they were just touring New Zealand. Thought they'd never seen enough of their own country. They hope to take a trip to Britain in years to come, and wanted to see all this first.'

Oh, how careful one had to be! It would never do to say it had been Dad's Moderatorial Year, visiting all the parishes. The name of the Moderator could easily leap to Rufus's mind. He probably had already connected it with this Eleanor St. John. She knew by now that the Sinclairs were Presbyterian. Marilla just loved the homestead chapel. It was interdenominational and had been consecrated by the Anglican and Roman Catholic Bishops of long ago, as well as blessed by ministers of all other denominations.

The first Sinclair wife had brought with her a young cousin and her husband, who had been of the Catholic faith, so the tiny chapel had been raised with that in mind. And all through the years with quite a number of the shepherds Catholic, or Anglican, or Methodist, the building had served them all.

'That way,' Marilla had said, 'is the best of all.'

Rufus had twinkled. 'It also gave us more services. A homestead as small as this couldn't expect a service here more than once in three months. I mean, it's up to us to go the thirty-odd miles into Wanaka, these days, with good cars, but when that road was little more than a track, it was good to have the service here. So with each denomination taking a quarterly service here, we average at least one a month. We all attended all the services of course, though the hands could please themselves, but it made us very ecumenically minded. And of course Father Lyon is a favourite with everybody.'

That night, with Jane leaning on Stephen's knee and small Anne perched on it, as he read them incidents long loved and familiar from one of Frederica Moorcroft's books, Marilla knew an almost overwhelming longing to tell Rufus, later that night, who she was.

This sort of setting, family life at its best, disarmed you. They'd seen all they wanted to, on the screen; Tony and Buck were playing chess. Evan and Coll, as befitted a Welshman and a Scot, were having an enjoyable wrangle on the respective merits of Rugby and Soccer, with Lindsay and Boyd egging them on, Rufus was busy at the table with farm papers. Marilla was knitting, of all things, an infinitesimal teddy-bear, for Anne's doll to cuddle in her pram. She had already finished one for Jane.

Stephen finished reading. Jane looked up, her delphinium blue eyes shining. 'Steve, tell us more about Frederica. Oh, I know you call her Elfreda, but we can't think of her as that. You *were* lucky knowing her. We don't know any real live authors.'

Rufus looked up and grinned. 'You make her sound like a real live tiger. And don't you think you've a nerve, calling a V.I.P. by his Christian name?'

Stephen looked reflective. 'V.I.P.? Oh, hardly that.'

'Well, you're attached to a Ministerial Department. That's nearly as good as being a Cabinet Minister yourself. And what amounts to a liaison officer between the conservationists and the power producers at that. If that's not important, what is?'

'I'm only important when I'm in the Capital, Rufe; when I was here I wasn't even a big frog in a little pool. I was of the lowest of orders, a rouseabout.'

They all stared. Lindsay said, 'Chief, that's not like you. It's almost snobbish ... you know, inverted snobbery. Those things don't matter to you.'

Marilla thought she might be imagining it, but Stephen's look seemed enigmatical, she thought.

He said, 'They don't matter to me now. They did then.'

Rufus looked puzzled. 'You can't mean my people made you feel that? I remember when you left here, Dad vowed you'd go a long way. Your hut was just lined with books, and what books! All unknown, you influenced my later reading considerably. I have all your books on my shelves.'

'Not your people. Though it happened about that

time that I ran into a bit of snobbery.'

Marilla spoke hotly. 'But people like that just aren't worth worrying about. They needn't mean a thing to anyone like you.'

Stephen's voice showed no resentment, just an acceptance. It had happened long ago, and he'd risen so high since it mustn't rankle any more.

'It needn't mean a thing if that attitude is of people casually and briefly met, but if it happens to be someone important to you, someone you hadn't dreamed could harbour such pettiness, then it can sting, especially when one is very young.' He laughed. 'My word, haven't we come a long way from reproving Jane? She did it so naturally, Rufe, then begged my pardon for it, so I told her to keep it up. It made me feel contemporary with young Boyd here, instead of an aged forty-five.'

Rufus said affectionately, 'Chump! I'm thirty-two myself. You may have seemed a lot older to me when I was a kid and you were bossing me around, but I've caught up a lot on you by now.'

Anne pulled Steve's sleeve impatiently. 'You promised to tell us about Frederica. What she looked like. Nanny told us a bit, once, and we've asked Mum and Uncle, but they're not very good at describing.'

Rufus looked insulted, then laughed. He said, 'Ask Guy and Marilla. They've seen her recently.'

Anne shook her head. 'We want to know what she was like when she was here.'

Stephen smiled reminiscently. 'She was very slender, so she looked tall but wasn't. She had a very quiet way of slipping about so you hardly noticed her, but she always reminded me of that saying about being careful ... "there's a chiel amang us taking notes." Because she used to wear great voluminous smocks over her slacks, with huge pockets. They sort of dwarfed her, but in the pockets she always carried a sketch-book. And suddenly you'd see her, say, sitting on that big sloping rock in that circle of lombardy poplars and aspens near where the new house is now, and she'd be busy lining something in.

'She was so quiet that once when I was watching her from Stalwart Crag, she was sitting on a fallen tree, and must've been there for ages, quite still, because I saw a couple of bunnies pop up from their holes and begin to play. We had far more rabbits then than now – in fact now there are none – but this fascinated me, so I didn't move myself. I was sure she'd seen them and had begun to sketch them. I thought even a movement from way up there might startle those bunnies.'

Jane and Anne both started to speak at once, but Stephen beat them to it, 'And this is it, the very afternoon in question,' and he picked up one of the books and opened it. There it was, just as he had said – the lombardies, so tall and symmetrical, the aspens that looked so real you could almost see them quiver, and the most adorable bunnies at play.

Anne's little pixie face quivered too. 'Isn't it a pity about rabbits ... that they're so beautiful, and so bad for the grazing?'

Jane nodded sagely. 'Granddad says that some runholders were eaten out by rabbits in the old days. Had to walk off their runs, ruined.'

Tony looked up from his chessboard. 'Good thing ponies and donkeys are nothing but good. Frederica draws them beautifully. That story where the children of Rainbow Hill bring the injured tramper in on the donkey's back is my favourite. It was old Saint Nicholas she used as a model. Mum and Uncle Rufus remember him.'

Stephen chuckled. 'Frederica learned to ride on the old Saint. She was so timid at first, then she got so fearless she used to scare seven bells out of us all. Never knew anyone have such a rapport with animals as she had. I can still see her picking her way down from the hillside above Leap Frog Falls. We'd never taken an animal up there. She had spotted a lamb stranded on a ledge on the far side. She was on Mirabel, Saint Nicholas's daughter. She'd been left alone at the homestead and had gone out sketching.

'She didn't realize we'd have done it on foot. But she saw the lamb was very weak. Just as well we didn't know she'd crawled out on that ledge. Good job it was too weak to struggle. I had nightmares at night for weeks thinking she might have crashed over. But we were coming back at the end of our muster, sweeping the hills for any stragglers, and I suddenly got the glasses focused on her. Certainly Mirabel was as sure-footed as a goat, but she had the lamb on the front of her. We hardly drew breath till she reached Tussocky Flat. Your grandfather told her off to a standstill.'

Rufus butted in. 'But he let that lamb live to a ripe old age. Said she was a symbol. What a nuisance she was! Imagined she was a lapdog, not a great big whopping ewe. I once found her curled up on my bed.'

Anne flicked over the well-thumbed pages 'Is this her? She called her Naughty Marietta? But there's nothing about that adventure here, and Granddad never told us that story.'

'*I* called her that,' said Stephen. 'Pity I hadn't had some nieces or nephews – I might have bought these books then and recognized them. I wouldn't have been able to resist writing to her.'

Guy said, 'You still could, Steve. I've got her address, of course. Think what a thrill she'd get to hear from someone who was here when she was. Come to think of it, I could take you to visit her when we finally make the Capital again.'

To their surprise, Steve shook his head decidedly. 'I think not. Too much water has flowed under the bridge since then.'

He looked down. One of the books lay open at the sketch of the stone seat that was captioned: *The Place-of-dreams-come-true.* He made a curiously caressing gesture, rubbing his thumb over it. Then, quite abruptly, he shut the book. 'It's a mistake to try to turn the clock back.'

Jane looked up from her footstool. The delicate oval of her face made Marilla long to have Elfreda's gift, to sketch it. Jane asked, 'Was it you who first called her Freddie?'

Stephen nodded. 'Yes. Elfreda seemed a mouthful.'

Jane nodded sagely, 'Then I expect that's why she chose Frederica for her pen-name.'

Out of the mouths of babes and sucklings, Marilla thought. Because suddenly she knew this was the man Elfreda had loved. She looked across at Stephen Ranaldson, his lean lantern-jawed face all angled shadows in the light from the standard lamp. This was the man Aunt Myrtle would have deemed her niece too good for. A mere rouseabout!

CHAPTER EIGHT

THERE were times when Marilla wished she could borrow a pair of legs off the cat. The moment she sat down to have a rest she got her eye on something else that needed doing.

Rufus took her to task. 'You're mad, Marilla. You're setting yourself impossible standards. What the heck does it matter if the kitchen floor's not swept every day, if the cottage verandah is cobwebby? Honestly, when I found you brushing the walls down with the yard broom today I could have spanked you! There's always more work here than Mother and Di can possibly manage, so they have to be sensible. That's why Di's keen to get a smaller, more convenient house.' His lips twitched in the now familiar way. 'That's probably why they're so dead keen to get me wed. I said I'd live on here, going over there for most meals, and shut some of this up when Mum and Dad retired. Why can't they leave it at that?'

Marilla looked about her. 'Perhaps they feel, as most women would, it'd be a crime to let this place go back.' She couldn't resist adding, 'So you ought to understand why they matchmake.'

'I could understand *their* feelings. It was the feelings of this Eleanor creature got me. Talk about cold-blooded planning!'

Marilla spoke with a heat that caused Rufus to raise his brows. 'You may be doing her a grave injustice. She may have been a catspaw. Perhaps this woman who was recommending her simply knew her preferences and passed them on. The girl herself may not have known there was a bachelor owner up here.'

Rufus waved an impatient hand. 'Oh, Marilla, *you* didn't hear them. *I* did. It was a very detailed conversation. Mother knew as much about that girl as if she'd actually been told these things by the girl herself.

Fair go, it was like one of these arranged marriages you read about. And this is New Zealand! I'd never believe that girl didn't know.'

Marilla felt despair rise up in her. There'd never be a way of disproving it, either.

He reverted to the original topic. 'All I want you to do, Marilla, is supervise the kids' lessons so that when we're in contact again and Diana and Donal can get back, their papers are ready to send up to Wellington. If you can keep the place reasonably tidy in the meantime and cook us plain, sensible meals, and keep us all on our toes, helping you when we can, that's all that's necessary. You'll come a cropper otherwise.'

She gave a shrug. 'I admit I'm so tired by nightfall, I can't stay awake long enough to read more than five minutes, but I rise like a giant refreshed every morning. One look out of the bedroom window into that little sheltered garden with Lantern Hill rising up beyond, and I'm rarin' to go. And it's not all drudgery, Rufus. Don't forget it's a novelty to me.'

He said, soberly enough, 'It mightn't always be a novelty.'

She said in much the same tone, 'But I'll be gone before it can wear off.'

Their eyes met. He said slowly, 'Will you, Marilla?'

She nodded. 'I have other responsibilities beyond this valley. Family ones. Ties of kindred.'

He considered that. 'I've got used to you being here. I forget you come from another, bigger world.' He paused in his task of topping up the kerosene lamps. 'A world that has Guy in it again, eh?'

'That, among other things.'

'Is he going to be in Wellington permanently, then?'

'Yes, he's staying. The office is there, of course, and his mother lives there.'

'Near you?'

'Very near.' An impish smile touched her lips, but he was intent on his task and didn't see it. 'Our mothers are what you might call inseparables.'

'Damn! I've spilt it after all. Don't *you* ever suffer from matchmaking? I can't see how two mothers as close as that could resist trying it on.'

'They've given me up as a bad job. They know marriage has no place in *my* scheme of things.'

He put the funnel down on the newspaper he'd spread, looked at her very curiously. 'Marilla, I seem to be out of touch with a woman's world. My instinct is leading me astray. Everything about you, your warm-heartedness, your way with the children, your slant on life as expressed in your little homilies to them now and then, upholds family life and delight in home, hobbies, reading, gardening, pets – oh, the lot. Which all adds up to womanliness. But the moment marriage is mentioned, you shy off.' She shrugged, continuing to push stuffing into two paradise ducks they had thawed. 'It's just I'm not personally interested.'

'Which could add up to the fact that you've not met the right man yet to – well – stir your pulses.'

Marilla managed a creditable laugh. 'Rufus, it would take more than a quickened pulse to make me think of marriage.'

He looked at her sharply, but she was threading a cooking needle and began to draw the skin together with quick stabs.

'Well, I'll cross the t's and dot the i's. It could add up to the fact you've not yet met that man to stir your pulses plus fire your imagination, stimulate your mind, provide kindred interests, in fact, to be a blend of lover, friend, husband, the sort of man you'd like to father your children. How's that?'

She didn't reply instantly because she couldn't.

He repeated it sharply. 'How's that?'

She swallowed. 'It sounds fine. Analytical but ideal.'

'*Is* that the reason, then? I feel it could be, because it's very likely a girl nearly twenty-eight is more apt to be discriminating, not easily bowled over. Maybe she'd even distrust her senses, her emotions. *Is* it just that you've not met the right man yet, Marilla?'

She'd never sewn birds for the roasting-dish with such meticulous care before. She kept her voice very steady. 'Well, sometimes things aren't just as equal as that, Rufus Sinclair. There can be obstacles. You *can* meet the man who is all those things, but it's not to say the way is clear.'

'You mean you *have* met someone who'd fill the bill?'

'Yes.'

'But it's not Guy?' It was a statement, not a question.

She said, 'Why should you be so positive about that?'

'Well, he went away for three years. And it's not as if there'd be any obstacle there. He's free.'

A crease appeared between her brows, then it smoothed out. Oh ... he thought she'd fallen in love with someone already married. She snapped off her thread, said, 'There, that's ready to be put in this afternoon. I hate to be rushed with that job. Tell me, Rufus, because there are still some oranges left, does everyone like orange sauce with duck or do some, like me, prefer apple?'

He laughed. 'They all like orange, except me. I prefer apple. If that doesn't add up to compatibility, what does?' He dropped the bantering tone, wiped his hands, came to stand beside her so closely she could feel his side against her side.

She moved away, said, 'Don't you dare get any trace of kerosene on my ducks!'

He moved after her. 'One experience doesn't have to colour a lifetime, Marilla. Few people remain true to their first loves. If it doesn't come to fruition, I mean. Sounds fine in storybooks, remaining constant to a memory. In real life it usually happens that if a woman, or a man, are thwarted, they turn to the next best, sometimes finding even greater happiness that way. Pity to waste such good home-making material, don't you think? I don't remember one instance of anyone remaining wedded to a dream.'

Marilla said, 'But some do, all their lives. For instance Frederica Moorcroft. Oh, listen to me. I've caught it off the children. I mean Elfreda Grant.'

'What about Elfreda?' It was Stephen Ranaldson, and

something in his voice deepened the conviction that was growing on Marilla daily.

Marilla gave him a look more frank than any she'd given Rufus. 'Rufus and I have been arguing about the rarity of people staying true to their first loves. I brought up the exception – Elfreda. She loved and lost. I happen to know that, but not who. She had two holy terrors for aunts. They kept her under, but suddenly she's free of their yoke. I don't know any details, because I left home on this holiday just after it happened.'

'Just after what happened?' Stephen asked.

'It sounds dramatic and almost impossible in this day and age, but then, as my father says, her aunts are something left over from the Victorian age. I think she'd suffered an old-fashioned broken heart. So she didn't care. She kept her love of horses and her children's books; in all other things, she just lived on the surface, outwardly acquiescent. Suddenly she found that the man she loved hadn't given her up too easily after all, that her older aunt had made mischief. Guy tells me he was staggered when he got back. She's a changed person. I think she probably imagines this man will have married long since. She may try to find out, I don't know, but her faith in him has come back. It was wonderful to see.'

She looked up from the ducks and gave Stephen Ranaldson an extremely speaking look. Rufus must have sensed something. He looked from one to the other.

As Stephen turned away Marilla said, 'Are you expecting another storm, Rufus? I thought the lamps were fairly full. I noticed them in the flower-room this morning.'

He nodded. 'We missed the forecast, as you know, but there's a snowy look out west.'

'So you think the lines may come down?'

'We play safe. We're always ready for a late snowfall. We've been known to have them in December. But I think there's one on its way.'

Sure enough snow was predicted in the high-country and even to low levels. Not that they needed telling by then, because the leaden sky was closing in, the air was snell, the temperature dropping.

It was a case of all hands on the hillsides, Tony included. Marilla felt a greenhorn beside the two girls who knew exactly what the women must do. She worked beside them, thankful she'd prepared that dinner in the forenoon while the children were busy on essays and needed only the occasional supervision.

They carried huge amounts of wheat and pollard from the sheds to the smaller storage bins in the fowlruns, draped scrim shelters over frameworks that protected the more frost-tender plants that were just beginning to appear in the garden; stocked up the donkey-house with plenty of hay in case they had to be driven inside, and helped one of the men clear the woolshed and bring hay inside.

Marilla was back inside when Stephen returned in the Rover to collect some gear the men wanted. He drank a steaming cup of coffee standing at the kitchen table. The girls were upstairs closing the sou'west shutters.

Stephen's keen blue eyes sought Marilla's. 'You've guessed it, haven't you? That Elfreda and I loved each other all those years ago?'

'Yes, a wild guess at first. I think it was the way you said her name. Stephen, I'm curious. Have you time to tell me what went wrong?'

'Yes, I've to meet them at Raggedy Point with that stuff, but they'll be ages getting there. Elfreda bowled me over, she was so sweet. Timid at first, but suddenly I was aware that there was more to her than on the surface. She seemed to bloom as time went on.' His glance went over Marilla's head into an infinity of remembering. Marilla knew that blooming would be when Elfreda found herself in love.

Stephen said, 'I found her rather reserved, except when she was with the children. Occasionally she'd forget herself, but then she'd draw into her shell again. I was afraid to force the pace. I was young, I had nothing to offer her, beyond a job on some homestead as a married couple.

126

That position here was filled. It mightn't have been as congenial, as beautiful. Years of saving for our own place lay ahead. I could tell she'd been gently reared. She taught music, and was taking art lessons. I felt rather – well, rough, beside her. But she didn't seem to notice. Not then.

'I played it along for a bit. Then one night as I came out of the tower where I'd been trimming the lantern – it wasn't electric then – she was sitting on that seat she sketched for a book. It was moonlight, not golden, but silver that night. It was so still even the leaves of the aspens weren't quivering. Everyone else was inside. There seemed to be only the two of us in all that vastness. I sat down and turned to her. She turned to me – and that was it.

'She was very reticent about her own life. I wanted to go up to Wellington to meet her family. She said two aunts had brought her up. I had no family to speak of. Some cousins somewhere. My father was killed in World War Two, in the islands. Mother died a few years later. It cut short my education. I was old enough to work, but had so little behind me. I was saving hard though, always dreaming of owning land in the high-country. When Elfreda knew it was time for her to go back, she changed, became distant. I was young enough to feel hurt, to show my resentment.'

Marilla said softly, 'She'd dread going back to her aunts. You've no idea what terrors they are, quite Gothic! She wouldn't want you to know what a coward she was about telling them. They'd tried to marry her off so many times, Dad said. To such lady-like men! She'd be afraid that they would hurt you.'

He looked grim. 'Instead of which, Marilla, Elfreda herself did the hurting.'

Marilla blinked. 'I can't under any circumstances imagine Elfreda doing that. Not purposely.'

'Well, she did. Quite frankly, I realized that once she knew her return was imminent, she was just plain ashamed of me. I said I'd take my holidays soon and go up north to meet the aunts. She put me off, not very skilfully. We had a fight. Oh, you probably can't imagine her fighting. It wasn't a bawling match, it was low and intense but it was very cutting. She begged me, finally, to give her time – time to get her aunts used to the idea. I blew up.'

Marilla's grey eyes were full of understanding. Of the young rouseabout blowing up. Of Elfreda's terror, not for herself, but lest Stephen be hurt. She would want to protect him.

Marilla said, 'If you can bear to, Stephen, you must tell me all your side of it.'

He took her hands, smiled down on her. Oh, but he was handsome! She could imagine how Elfreda had loved him, how scared she had been. Pity she hadn't married him in Wanaka and just announced it to the aunts. They would have reacted typically ... forbidden her their house and told her she'd made her bed and could lie on it. And she would have been supremely happy with a man like this.

Stephen said, 'This morning when you said the aunts had made mischief, what *could* you mean? You said Elfreda had found out. What did she have to find out? It was Elfreda's own attitude that defeated me.'

'They made mischief somehow. You've no idea what they're like. Entirely selfish.'

He said, unexpectedly, 'But I do know what they're like. I met them later. I wrote to Elfreda telling her I was coming up to Wellington, apologizing for losing my temper, and that I wanted to meet her aunts, even if they might not find me what they'd hoped for, with regard to their niece. But she wouldn't even see me. She ran away, wouldn't meet me. And to be quite candid the aunts were rather nice to me – unexpectedly so. Marilla, don't look so astounded. You're positively gaping. They really were.'

'I just can't believe it! If they were, then it was the smile on the face of the tiger. You know ... with the lady inside him. Oh ... had Elfreda not told them you were just a rouseabout? Did they think you were the son of the

128

homestead or something?'

'They knew exactly who I was, no doubt of that. They even seemed a little troubled that their niece should have been so immature and rude as to have gone off to a Pacific island and left them to tell me she couldn't marry me.'

'She never did!' ejaculated Marilla fiercely. 'Never! Not Elfreda. She wouldn't. This is where something went wrong. Tell me exactly how it happened.'

'Well, I thought I should take the bull by the horns. I said I truly loved their niece. That, as they seemed to know, I'd written saying sorry for all the stupid things I'd said, and wanted to meet her aunts. They were both embarrassed and kind.'

'Kind?' the word was positively jerked out of Marilla.

'They said they were very sorry, that Elfreda should have waited and told me herself, but they were afraid that because she had been orphaned, they had rather spoiled her. She couldn't face telling me it had just been infatuation, that our circumstances were just too different. So she'd asked them to tell me when I came, and she'd gone off to Norfolk Island.'

Comprehension of that last detail leapt into Marilla's eyes. 'That at least was a lie, Stephen. She wasn't running away from you when she went to Norfolk. We all know why Elfreda once went there long ago, because the friends she went to live quite near her in Wellington. I mean, it's not just something I heard when I was a tiny child.

'Elfreda had a friend she loved very much, an older girl, who had championed a very lonely, shy wee girl, at the select private school she'd been sent to. She's Olwen Grenwick. She and her husband and little girl were holidaying on Norfolk. He went out fishing and was drowned. Olwen's mother had arthritis and wasn't very mobile. But she wanted to go to her daughter. Elfreda offered to accompany her on the flight. She looked after the little girl while the wife and mother attended to all the arrangements. This must have been what Elfreda meant, that she'd found out you'd come and gone, and she'd never been told.'

'But what about the letter? Why didn't she write? I grovelled. I felt I'd been too hard on her, that she'd been brought up gently and I'd terrified her with my anger. But when she didn't answer, I had to accept the fact that she knew it just wouldn't work. A few months later I worked my passage to Britain.'

Marilla said, 'I should very much like to know if she ever got that letter. I wouldn't put it past Aunt – past her Aunt Myrtle to have seen the letter, read it, then destroyed it. I'd just like to know. If Elfreda found that out, no wonder she changed. So don't you think she *ought* to know what really happened all those years ago? She may not know the full story even yet. Stephen, perhaps I'm rushing in with spiked boots where angels wouldn't even tiptoe, but don't you think she deserves to know that you wrote? Or is this just my love of a happy ending? They tell me at home I'm an incurable romantic. Perhaps you don't want to – er—'

He was still holding her hands. 'Have another go? Oh, but I do. Marilla, do you ever have the feeling that Fate takes a hand in our affairs? I feel I was meant to come here, to find you, and through you to hear about Elfreda.'

A voice broke in, trying to sound severe. 'And I suppose *I'm* to think it a good thing that a river changed its course, that we're going to be cut off for weeks, that it will hold up our sale of fat lambs, that the kids' parents can't get home by orthodox means . . .?'

They swung round, embarrassed. Rufus, stern-visaged, was in the doorway, his red hair bright against it.

They both rushed into speech, trying to explain. They stopped as he gave a guffaw. 'It's okay. I heard almost the lot. I've had my suspicions for some time that your interest in Elfreda's books meant more than it seemed at first. And I vaguely remember from my boyhood that you were often together. It's okay, Steve. I just hope we ride this storm out, and you meet up soon with your Elfreda, Steve.'

Steve had dropped Marilla's hands, but now he caught them again, and kissed her, quite heartily, full on the mouth, and went out, clapping Rufus on the shoulder and saying, 'Thanks a lot. Jove, I'd better get cracking!'

Marilla, embarrassed for what reason she knew not, said, 'Would you like some coffee, Rufus?'

Rufus came across, tall, broad, in a heavy jersey, laughed, said, 'No, I'd rather have what he's just had,' seized her, kissed her, then as Anne and Jane erupted into the kitchen, let her go so abruptly, she had to steady herself by the table-edge.

But he hadn't been quick enough. They stopped, clapped their hands over their mouths to stop the excited squeals that were imminent from bursting out of them. They solemnly surveyed Marilla and Rufus, their mouths hidden, but their blue eyes dancing with delight.

Then it was too much for them. The hands fell and they giggled madly. Anne looked saucy. 'Are you going to get married, then?' Before either Marilla or Rufus could reply, Jane said, a blissful look on her face, '*Won't* Mum be pleased! *And* Nanny. Mum said to her it would solve all her problems if only you'd get married, Uncle Rufus.'

Their uncle spread out his hands in a hopeless gesture. 'See,' he said to Marilla, 'See how I get trapped? Four females in this household, Di, Mother, Jane and Anne. All minds with but one single thought: Get Rufus married.'

The joy on the two small faces faded a little. Jane said, eyes clouding, 'You don't mean you aren't—?'

Marilla was sure Rufus would make a hash of it. She said, quickly, 'Your uncle was only fooling, girls. That wasn't – er – a serious kiss.'

Anne muttered something under her breath.

Her uncle said sharply, 'Speak up, let's all hear it if you have anything to say.'

She said airily, 'I said I thought it looked a pretty good one to me.'

He said sarcastically, 'And who made you an authority on kisses?'

Anne could always hold her own. She said defiantly, 'I've got my imagination, haven't I?'

Rufus snorted, 'A lot of good that is. Imagination isn't experience.'

Marilla bit her lip in an endeavour not to laugh, the next moment. Jane was sometimes unexpected. 'I don't know,' she said, in the most mature fashion. 'We were having this talk about what we wanted to do when we grew up. Anne said she'd be a writer. Dad said she'd better train for something else first, because writers needed scads of experience and they had to earn their living first. But Mum said not always, that she'd just read in a book that imagination isn't just making up, it's finding out.'

Rufus looked bewildered. 'You've lost me. Anyway, I'm preparing for a snowstorm, not proposing marriage to your governess.'

Jane wasn't going to be diverted like that, from such a fascinating topic. 'It was a funny time to be kissing, then, wasn't it?'

Marilla decided it was up to her to rescue Rufus. 'I told you it was in fun. It was because he came in just as Mr. Ranaldson kissed me, so—'

'Steve?' cried Anne. 'Kissing *you*? Why, he's as old as anything. Marilla, you wouldn't—'

'Girls! We are *not* talking of marriage. I happened to – er – help Steve about something, so he kissed me for it. Nothing in it. Now that's enough. There's something to be said for boys. You don't catch Tony talking about kissing and marriage all the time. Did you get all the shutters fastened? And clamp the catch on the toilet louvres? Good. Now if the men haven't any other chores lined up for us, we'll whip round the garden and pick as many flowers as we can. If it snows, they'll be flattened out.'

Anne, slightly squashed, said gloomily, 'Nothing romantic ever happens here. We've never had an engagement, a wedding, nothing. And I need it for copy.'

Rufus, departing, said over his shoulder, 'Better stick to pixies and elves and hidden treasure for a few years. We're a prosaic family, poppet. But let me warn you about one thing. . . . If ever I do propose to a girl, it won't be in front of my nieces. You can get your copy from someone else.'

The men worked till the mountain twilight struck in. At Green Gables they lost the sun much earlier than over at Lantern Hill.

The bleating of lambs and ewes temporarily separated filled the air, dogs were barking, calves bawling, cattle lowing. One was conscious of a world of animals, of movement. Marilla was glad when all the men were safely in. How soon this had become her world. She looked round the enormous table, the three children, herself, and eight men, and felt a zest of the spirit never before known.

Here were stable things, here Magnus and Morag Sinclair had come, braving the wilderness, the unbridged rivers, the mountain fastnesses. Every tree other than the forest trees belonged to the Sinclairs, planted as tiny saplings, some even from cones; every rock on the garden terraces had been gouged out of their hillsides and sledged down to be landscaped into the garden, to keep the pockets of soil from slipping down the slopes.

She brought her smiling gaze back to encounter Rufus's very intent look. She felt he had read her very thoughts and was horrified to find a blush rising. Good heavens, as a school-ma'am of quite some years, she thought she was past that. Rufus didn't look away, he kept a little smile round his lips. Marilla hurriedly disengaged her eyes only to encounter Anne and Jane exchanging meaning grins. She reached out as if she needed salt. Anne's thin little fingers seized her wrist as she began to sprinkle, 'Marilla, that's caster sugar, not salt!'

'Oh, how stupid of me, whatever made me do that?' Then she turned her shoulder on the girls as they dissolved into giggles.

'Girls!' said Tony in disgust. 'What they find to giggle about is beyond me.'

Marilla didn't want any probing on that score. She said

hastily, 'Oh, look, the first snowflake drifting past the window.' Then she said, 'Children, we'll leave the dishes. I'm going to get you into the schoolroom to do an hour and a half on your lessons. Because I can see you'll all be wanted outside tomorrow.'

CHAPTER NINE

MARILLA found when she came back from the time in the schoolroom, and had supervised baths and had a story-time with the girls, that the men had not only stacked the washer, but had the dishes all washed, dried, and put away. They were still in the kitchen. 'Thought we'd stay in here tonight,' said Steve. 'It's getting colder and even with the central heating we'd need a fire in the lounge. That would mean ashes for you to deal with tomorrow.'

They had the huge old-fashioned enamel coffee-pot on the stove, green, flecked with white, and cookies out and mugs. Guy said, 'We've planned to wait on you tonight. That was a tremendous dinner you cooked for us, in addition to everything you did outside, Sis.'

Sis. Marilla froze.

Rufus, in a deep winged chair, turned his head sideways and looked at Guy who was quite unaware. 'Sis? I've never heard you call her that before.'

Nothing could set Guy back. He said easily, 'Haven't used it for years. When I was small I couldn't get my tongue round r's and l's, you see. So Marilla was beyond me. So I called her Sis.'

Rufus said, 'Why? I don't see the connection. My sister, now, had that trouble, and called me Woof. I felt more like a collie dog than a human being. Kathleen it was.'

Guy said, poker-faced, 'They tried me with her second name, Cecilia. Sis was the nearest I could get to that one.'

'You lived near each other, I think you said.'

'So near we grew up just like brother and sister. I even saw her have her first bath.'

Marilla choked. 'Guy, don't be such a liar! That bit of walnut cookie went down the wrong way! You're outrageous. You couldn't remember that, I was born in a nursing-home.'

'Well, your first bath after you were brought home. And of course I remember it. After all, it was a revelation to me. Till then I'd thought the only difference between girls and boys was buttons and bows.'

Marilla choked again. 'Guy!'

'Now, no more reminiscences. There are distinct drawbacks to having someone round who knew one from the word go. Believe me, I could drag up some pretty embarrassing stories about you, but I've got too nice a nature.'

The phone rang.

Di, from Auckland. She'd come in from hospital to hear a Dominion-wide forecast and, like them all, feared disruption of telephonic communication. Donal was much better, though they were not discharging him yet. And when they did, their Auckland friends wanted them to stay till he could travel without setback.

Rufus said, 'Well, even when the snow clears keep him up there as long as possible. Have the time of your life, Di, when Donal's able to get about. Live it up for a change. Our Miss Sinjin is at the helm, a holy terror for discipline, has even made the kids do an extra hour and a half to-night because they'll be outside tomorrow for sure, feeding out. She's as tough as an old boot herself. Good as a landgirl. Perhaps she was one, way back in World War Two.

'Anyway, don't worry about us. With old Britannia at the helm, nothing can us dismay. That's what the kids have named her, and no wonder. Night-night.'

He put the phone down and looked vastly pleased with himself.

Marilla said faintly, 'Between you and Guy I hardly recognize myself. Dippy, that's what you are, clean dippy!'

Stephen said, 'What was all that about? I'm in the dark.'

Buck, Coll, and Evan caught on and doubled up with laughter. 'We've got it! Steve, Rufus has an awful time dodging the matchmakers. Fair go, his mother and sister are holy terrors. The nights poor Rufus has had to come over to our quarters and play cards to dodge some girl Di's asked out here to say are countless! He's terrified they'll make up their minds this is it, cut off with a ravishing redhead!'

Marilla surveyed them coldly. 'There was no need to go to all that nonsense. He's completely and utterly safe from *this* redhead, believe me. Now it *is* going to be a case of off to bed.'

The phone rang again. Guy said, 'That'll be your lady mother, Rilla, having heard the forecast.' It was. Marilla knew panic, but Elfreda must have primed her well, because she asked no questions to which answers might be awkward.

Marilla said, 'So you realize we could be cut off. Pet, it's been horrid not being able to write to you, but I've written a page or two every day describing life here to you – it will remind you and Dad of your days in the Mackenzie country. When we can get out of here again, I'll post it to you. Though with being here so long, I may not go down to Fiordland as planned, I may just come home.'

A hand wrested the phone from her, Rufus's. Marilla made an unavailing clutch. Whatever would Mother say to him? Rufus said, 'Ah, Mrs. Sinjin, it's Rufus Sinclair here. We don't particularly want your daughter leaving here when we get access. We need a governess pretty badly. How about you coming here for a holiday when that happens? You'd be having them in January, I suppose? If we weren't connected by then with a swing bridge or something, wouldn't you like the novelty of coming in by chopper? I can assure you we'd love to have you. No, it wouldn't be too much for my sister. When they do come home they'll move to the new house. Marilla would have to cook for you.

'And if you'd like to make it a family affair, all the better. Marilla tells me she has a young brother and sister at Varsity. Might they like up-country jobs during vacation like so many do? We can always do with extra hands.'

Marilla felt her hands go clammy. She made gestures to Rufus to hand the phone back. He said, 'I'll let you talk it out with Marilla, she's trying to grab the phone off me. I expect she thinks I'm costing you a fortune, going on like this.'

Marilla got the earpiece up in time to hear her mother say reprovingly, 'Marilla, how ungracious of you, dear, when that charming young man was issuing such a generous invitation.'

'Yes,' said Marilla vaguely. 'What a pity you've got that cruise booked. But you could possibly see this place some other time. And of course, while Kit and Fiona would have jumped at it most years, they're off with that team to New Caledonia for French study, aren't they?'

'What?' gasped her mother.

Marilla prattled on. 'Yes, yes, I agree. The chance of a lifetime for them. But it was very kind of Mr. Sinclair to offer. Mother, would you pass on a message to Elfreda? Did you happen to hear on the news that the leader of this section Guy was seconded to was a Mr. Stephen Ran-aldson? Elfreda may have missed that bit of news. He worked up here when she was here all those years ago. I thought she might be interested.' She caught Stephen's eye. 'What? Not in Wellington? Then where is she? Down the South Island? Well, if she happens to ring you, or write, tell her. Give Dad my love. And I'm sure Guy, who's looking at me, wants me to give you his too. 'Bye—' But once again the phone was snatched from her.

Guy said, 'Hullo, Aunt Helena. It's your favourite courtesy nephew here. I was going to ring my own mother to say we might be cut off, so perhaps you'll do it for me. Yes, it seems unreal to me, finding Marilla here. Talk about Sydney and the bush — I keep telling myself that only six weeks ago I was in Edinburgh, and now I'm marooned beyond the foothills. Never mind,' he winked audaciously at Marilla, 'it gave your beautiful daughter and myself a chance to take up again where we left off. Bye-bye, Aunty.' And to Marilla's great relief he hung up.

Evan looked at Coll. 'Just our luck, to get someone like

Marilla on the property, and have a boy-friend from her past drop in out of the skies. Toss you for the privilege of seeing her home, Guy . . . nice night for a saunter.'

They could hear the soft hiss of snowflakes against the panes and they were piling up on the sills. They began scattering for bed.

There was no gale, just a gentle, non-stopping smothering blanket of snow, hour after hour.

Marilla woke at two, conscious of a light. She grabbed her dressing-gown and slippers, investigated. Tony's light. He was in bed, staring up at the ceiling. Tony, ninety per cent of the time, was tough and self-sufficient. But not tonight. She went in, said quietly, 'Are you all right? Can't you sleep? Have you a pain anywhere?'

He looked so glad to see her, Marilla's heart warmed. She was relieved when he said no pains. 'I woke up, Marilla, and I got to thinking.' She thought his voice had a faint sniff.

She said, 'So did I. Can I get under your eiderdown?' He nodded. She slid under, pulled it well round her shoulders. The girls were more used to expressing their feelings.

She said, 'I felt a bit blue tonight too, and woke up still feeling down. My mother rang tonight when she heard the forecast. I've been too busy here to miss Mum and Dad, but it sort of swept over me that I haven't seen them for a while. Did you feel that way too?'

'Sure did. Mum's such fun. She's the one with the Irish streak in her, Dad says. Uncle Rufus and Aunt Kathy are more like Granddad. Nanny was born in Dublin and came out here when she was twelve, with her parents. She still has that way of putting things, and so has my mum. Everything that happens up here is fun to Mum. Do you think I'm sissy for missing her?'

Marilla said gravely, because a boy's opinion of himself was a serious matter, 'Hardly. If I, a schoolteacher of twenty-seven, can miss my mother, even allowing for the fact that I'm a girl, that makes me more than twice your age. I'm not even very demonstrative, I just like her round, that's all.'

Tony said, 'Gee, I'm glad you didn't say: "Come on, cheer up now. Put a stiff upper lip on it." I hate being cheered up!'

'So do I,' said Marilla fervently. 'When I'm feeling blue, which isn't very often, but it's a real navy-blue when I am, I like to simply wallow!'

Tony chuckled and a voice from the shadows of the hall said, 'Would you mind if I came in and wallowed with you? Though I don't think we'd better yowl, or we'll wake everyone up.'

Rufus, in dressing-gown, sat on the other side of the bed. 'I was feeling low too, so I thought I'd come down and make myself some chocolate. How about if I got us all some? It's the last straw, a late snowfall on top of the Waihemo busting through to the Blue! And to be quite candid, I miss like the devil being able to write to Mum and Dad and get letters from them. Oh, I know we'll get an enormous bunch of mail all at once – I expect if this lasts, our marooning, I mean, they'll bring mail and stores in by helicopter – but it's not the same as getting it every two or three days.'

Tony said, 'I didn't think grown-ups ever felt quite like that.'

'Chump, of course they do. We hide our feelings, that's all. We like to think we can take it, that we're tough. So here goes, let's have a real grizzle. I think it's positively rotten that the river burst its banks.'

Tony came in, 'And that Dad had to get peritonitis when he was in Auckland. That we've got snow just when they could get over the Bailey bridge on the Motatapu and inspect *our* road.'

They looked at Marilla. They were expecting her to say: 'That we're so isolated, that we may even lose our phone, that it makes more and more work,' but she couldn't. She loved this isolation. She loved being cooped up here with the children, with ... Rufus. She didn't want to leave Blue Canyon ever, but when the snows melted and the surveyors got busy and rigged up some sort of access, and Donal MacGillivray was well enough for him and Diana to be flown in, there'd be a reckoning, an exposure.

Rufus would be furious because he'd been made to look such a fool. And she didn't think he'd ever believe she hadn't been in the matchmaking from the start. He'd said so. Even if Diana backed her up, the fact that his men would know he'd been deceived, that his nephew and nieces would laugh their heads off, would all go against her. She'd lost her chance of explaining, long ago. Each day had worsened the situation. But she still couldn't explain. Not when the house was full of strangers, when none of them could get away from the others ... she couldn't risk creating disharmony when it wasn't possible to explain, and depart ...

Besides which, she didn't want to do anything now that might upset in any way her chance, slender though it was, of bringing Elfreda and Stephen together. That mattered far more than her own ultimate discomfiture.

These thoughts, which had kept her company all day, just flashed through her mind now, but even so, Rufus and Tony were looking at her, waiting for her to say her piece.

She grinned, and said, over the eiderdown hugged up to her neck, 'But apart from missing our parents like heck, poor things that we are, it's great fun, isn't it?'

Tony gave a muffled chuckle, said, 'You beaut, Marilla! I said Mum was fun, and so're you.'

Rufus leaned over and slapped the place on the eiderdown where her knee should be, said, 'Sport!' Now I'll go and make that hot drink. Don't make too much noise, we don't want the lassies to wake up.'

They giggled silently at his tray. 'It's a real midnight feast, isn't it?' whispered Tony. 'Pavlova and hot chocolate!'

'Well,' said Rufus excusingly, 'I knew there was just that much left over from those whopping pavs you made yesterday, Marilla. I just can't resist pavs.'

They were enormous wedges, with the pavlova faintly crisp and sugary on the outside, filled simply with pineapple, cream, and passion-fruit pulp. The hot chocolate was delicious.

Tony cuddled down immediately afterwards. Rufus said, 'For once I won't be a spoil-sport and insist on you cleaning your teeth again – come on, Marilla.'

They left the tray and walked out to the still warm passage where one dim light burned. They paused. He looked at her. The only dressing-gown she had with her was an inadequate affair of apricot brushed nylon. It fell open over her emerald green fluffy nightgown, like a redingote. Her luxuriant hair, softly curling at the ends, fell forward over her face for once.

He said, 'Where ever did you get that extraordinary garment? It's an evening dress, isn't it? Did you think it would be warmer?'

She laughed, the creases deepening each side of her mouth. Her lips parted over the irregular teeth that gave such an endearingly crooked twist to her smile. 'It belongs to your mother. The girls said Di brought it from Canada for her. I've got a cheek, I know, but I had such flimsy pyjamas with me.'

Rufus said, 'I must suggest Mother gives it to you, as a token of gratitude for holding the fort for us here, in kitchen and schoolroom. It's perfect on you.'

Marilla said with spirit, 'You'll do nothing of the kind. Your mother would want to know how you'd seen it on me. It would take some explaining, believe me.'

The corners of his mouth quirked upwards. 'It would, I suppose. Hadn't thought of that – just of how you look in it. Just a moment, you've got a blob of cream on your cheek, making you look like a little girl at a party. And about ten with your hair like that.'

He dived his hand into his dressing-gown pocket, brought out a handkerchief, took a step forward and caught her elbow to steady her. He wiped the cream off, then stood still. His face was serious.

Marilla felt she ought to move, but couldn't. What had

come over her?

Rufus said, 'You're quite free to say no, if you like, Marilla, but I should very much like to kiss you. I don't really believe kisses ought to be snatched ... they ought to be given, each to each ... shared. Twice before, I've taken you unawares, and each time you've resented that. But I'm wondering. I mean – oh, hang it, I'd better come straight out with it. I asked once before, but I've not been sure since ... does Guy Stewart mean anything big in your life? I mean romantically. Do you care for him? I'm not one to poach on anyone else's preserves. And he's a good chap.'

Marilla was at a loss. Her own feelings were tumultuous. She'd never felt – quite – like this in her life. This might clear the ground a little. Perhaps it wasn't as hopeless a situation as she had dreaded.

She looked up, the grey eyes clear and steady for once. 'I'm not in the least in love with Guy, Rufus. Neither, for that matter, is he in love with me. It's quite a different type of affection. But he loves to tease. So—'

He took that one step nearer, his eyes alight. 'So ... that's consent. Good. I couldn't stand a repeat of those other two kisses. Let's make this a good one.'

He put his hand out, one each side of her throat, and lifted the hair up from her face, pushing it to the back. Then he slid his arms round her, bent his head, looked very briefly, but rather searchingly into her eyes, with the faintest of smiles playing round that well-cut mouth of his, swung her a little sideways, and put everything he had into that kiss.

So did Marilla. She had no idea how long it lasted. She only knew she didn't want it to end, that it filled her with hope, with promise for future understanding. He lifted his mouth from hers, put the side of his cheek, faintly rough, against the side of hers, holding her against him still. But when at last she stirred and put a faint pressure on his arms to release her, he slackened his grip immediately, as if her wishes were his.

She said, a little shakily, 'Rufus, I must go. Imagine if

anyone – Stephen, for instance – came downstairs and—'

He laughed and ruffled her bright head. 'I know. It could never be explained away. It would look shameless. To explain would be to accuse ourselves and it would spoil that moment for us. Lots of situations in life like that, of course, and we're so inclined to put the wrong construction on them. Good-night, Rilla, pleasant dreams.'

As she drifted off to sleep in a haze of happiness, she thought, smilingly, that it was the first time he had ever used the diminutive of her name.

CHAPTER TEN

THE next day had no leisure moments, no tender incidents. But there was one magical one, just the same, when they first crowded into the kitchen to look out across Lantern Hill and the rolling stuff beyond the old bed of the Waihemo.

Marilla knew she mustn't breathe: 'How exquisite!' when there could be such stock losses, such heavy work, days of fighting the elements to come, but, surprisingly, Rufus said it for her. 'Could anything be more beautiful?' Then, being a practical man, 'Or more deadly?'

Marilla laughed. 'I was afraid to comment on it. I thought any expression of admiration would sound like a thoughtless utterance from an idealistic city dweller.'

Coll burst out laughing. 'Listen to her, every inch a schoolmarm! I couldn't put a sentence like that together to save my life.'

Marilla looked surprised. 'What? You do yourself an injustice, Coll. In the letter I keep writing to my mother, in the hope of being able to post it some day, I happen to have said your vocabulary fascinates me. You have an instinctive choice of descriptive and dramatic words and you never um and aah.'

Coll was hushed into surprised silence, but looked pleased.

Marilla said crisply, 'Now, let's at it. I slipped down early, before any of you stirred, and put the lights on because the shutters were still up, and got things going. Nobody need help dish out this morning. I'll keep you all supplied and have mine after. Just get outside the moment you have something warm inside you.'

She added, 'I'll be with you as soon as I get the soup made and a casserole in. They can be left to cook for themselves then.'

Rufus said, 'It's hard work, and you won't be used to it,

though anybody's boots treading out a path to the sheep helps, even the dogs' feet do, but—'

'Look, when we lived at Fairlie, we were out on one of the big stations up Mount Cook way when they had a late fall. We were only kids, but we thought it was marvellous, being allowed to help. We had a great time, didn't we, Guy?'

Too late, she realized what she'd said. The other night Rufus had said to Guy, 'How come you were neighbours in Fairlie and now your mother lives near Marilla's folk in Wellington?' Unfortunately Guy had said, 'Well, my people lived in Fairlie about the time Marilla was born – I told you they met at a clan reunion in Timaru and discovered they lived in the same town – but when I was small my people moved to Wellington, and later Marilla's father accepted a call to a parish there.'

So now Marilla added lamely, 'Guy was on holiday with us.'

Rufus said, 'Holiday? And it was a *late* fall? How come? Holidays are August and May and January.'

Guy came in. 'I was recuperating after being sick. They sent me to Aunt Helena's for convalescence. Marilla and I were at this station for the weekend and got marooned there for much longer. It was this time of year all right.'

Rufus seized another piece of toast, reached out for the apple jelly. 'What station was it?'

'Ben Argyll. Up beyond Simon's Pass.'

'Oh, the Forbes' place? I was at Waitaki Boys' High with Ian Forbes. Same year, same dormitory. You'd know him, then?'

'Yes,' said Marilla. 'Not that he was home at that time. I was still at Primary, of course.' Oh dear, now they had mutual friends. Some day her two worlds would come together and crash. How much better it would be if she could get away from here before Donal and Di came home. Yet she wouldn't be able to leave the children, even if they got a helicopter in. But for that responsibility she'd have pretended an urgent call home.

Suddenly she hated all this. Lying destroyed one's

confidence. You lost all your openness, your sense of integrity. It made you unnatural, and put a frightful strain on your memory. Once you told a lie you had to tell another. There was that children's talk Dad gave, about a lie having no legs. It has to be propped up. All at once Marilla made up her mind that as soon as possible she'd tell Rufus. That she'd been so set back when he'd roared at her for coming in with a tiny car and having no mechanical knowledge, she'd decided the job wasn't for her and she'd leave Blue Canyon without him being any the wiser.

That a bigger shock had hit her when he asked her to write that letter and explained why. And that he *must* believe she was *running away* from men, not *pursuing* them. And she'd have to explain that TV interview that had triggered it all off. Marilla found she'd put the grated carrots in the casserole and the sliced ones in the soup. Now she'd have to fish each lot out and transfer them. She'd better stop thinking about her own snarled-up affairs and get out into that incredibly beautiful and disastrous world outside, where animals might be in distress.

After lunch, Rufus said, 'Steve, I wonder if you'd give Marilla a hand for a bit? I'd like you both out again as soon as possible, but I don't want to have to stop myself to saw that meat up. Would you do it?'

Steve and Marilla worked at speed. She said, 'I can make a quick pudding when we come in at nightfall, and I won't peel potatoes, I'll just scrub them now and put them in that very slow oven. I don't want anyone so hungry they want supplementary bread with their dinner. I wish I'd done potatoes for lunch – they ate so much bread after all that work. It's running short. Making bread entails staying in to rise and knead it, so I'll just make a couple of Irish soda loaves tonight, to spin it out. Mum used to do this whenever we got unexpected visitors over the week-end, which was pretty often.'

Stephen was hacking into the mutton. 'Yes, it would be. I remember Guy saying the same thing once. We went over to Ireland and our landlady made some. He told her it had often been a godsend in the Manse.'

'It certainly had,' agreed Marilla, then, 'Oh! Oh, Steve, how did you—'

He burst out laughing. 'I've known some time. Guy and I mostly talked business. With the exception of that trip to the Irish lakes, we were hardly ever together apart from the projects, so I didn't know he had a sister Marilla. Or a half-sister, is that it? He once mentioned that his stepfather was a minister, and his name was St. John, but he certainly didn't call it Sinjin. I've been piecing it together bit by bit. Not that I can get the strength of it, or imagine why.

'But there was something else. Every time I look at you, I see something of Elfreda in you. There's a connection, isn't there? I recall Freddie saying once she had a cousin in the church. In your ways you couldn't be more different, Elfreda was so shy, so diffident, and you're all life and go, but in the turn of your head, and the lift of your eyebrow and the curve of your lips, I see her.'

Marilla said, 'You must think it mighty odd – and it is, come to that, but it's an awfully long story, and—'

'Aye, lassie. And you can't do it justice in the middle of a snowfall with all hands needed on deck. It can wait. You'll have your reasons and I'd stake my life on their being good ones.'

She said, miserably, 'They're very foolish ones. Oh, at the time when I concealed my identity, I didn't think I'd be here longer than the time it would take to fix my car. Oh, if only I'd time to tell you the events that led to me clearing out from Wellington, but I haven't.'

Stephen plonked the leg and forequarter into the two roasting-pans, and, from long experience, knifed dripping all over them. 'It's okay, Marilla – whatever you did it for would be only foolishness, nothing shady, that I do know.'

She clasped her hands together. 'Oh, Stephen, you do understand, if only Rufus will too!'

Stephen gave her a wry smile. 'I wasn't very understanding with your kinswoman all those years ago.

Perhaps I'm trying to make up for that now. Marilla, if Rufus is cross, don't take it too seriously – I think he will be, he'll feel a fool, but he'll get over it. There, into the oven.'

The phone rang just as Marilla was stabbing the scrubbed potatoes all over. She said, 'Stephen, answer that. I'm scared to, in case it's Di.'

He said, 'Blue Canyon Homestead here. Steve Ranaldson speaking.' Then his voice changed so much, Marilla swung round from the oven. He said, 'Elfreda . . .? Yes, it *is* Elfreda, isn't it? By all that's holy, where are you, girl?'

Marilla knew she should have folded her tent like the Arabs and silently stolen away, but she didn't. She couldn't. She was rooted to the spot.

He listened. 'At Bridget Granville's? Yes, of course I remember her. I always liked her, Freddie. Elfreda, it would *have* to happen like this, wouldn't it, now I've caught up with you again, that we're cut off from each other by a river rushing through where it's no business to be, and now a snowfall! There's more coming too, by the latest forecast. Otherwise I'd have ordered you to fly in here by helicopter. Did you hear that, girl? I said ordered. You're not getting away from me this time.

'Elfreda, you know Marilla's here, of course, doing a splendid job. She's helped me sort things out. She guessed. I couldn't hide it. Though not till I got here and Diana's children got me to read to them did I know you'd written books. Freddie, they're just magnificent, and just you. If only I'd come across them overseas!

'Married? No, of course I'm not married. Wouldn't be talking this way if I was. I've only ever loved one woman, and you can work out who for yourself. Listen, I know Marilla's working here incognito, but I've not had time to find out quite why yet – she and I agreed a few moments ago that she'll tell me when we've done a bit more rescue work on the stock. But as far as you and I were concerned, she knew enough to tell me the aunts had made mischief, that you hadn't gone to Norfolk Island because you hadn't the courage to tell me you couldn't face marrying a rouseabout – as your Aunt Myrtle told me when I called – that you'd gone because a friend had been bereaved there.

'You see, Elfreda, I'd written to you saying I was coming – Marilla thinks you may not have got that letter. I grovelled, Elfreda, for losing my temper like that, for letting my stinking pride get in the way. *Did* you get it, Elfreda? I say, are you there? Elfreda, are you there? Oh, Freddie, you've *got* to be there! Elfreda . . .?'

His voice changed, his shoulders sagged, he stood, holding the phone, turned to Marilla. She knew then, by the real despair in his voice, his eyes, how much he loved her cousin. 'Marilla . . . the line's gone. It's – it's as dead as a dodo. Oh, pray God we're only cut off, that it *doesn't* mean the line's gone. Look, an operator could have pulled the plug out by mistake.'

But it was no good. They waited longer than they should have, with the work on the hill waiting them. They tried to dial the Wanaka exchange, and their nearest neighbour. To no avail.

Marilla flew to him as he stood there defeated. 'Don't look like that. She got the message – that you still love her. They'll get the line going again.'

'If only that break is near Wanaka, not back here. But I'm afraid it's more likely to be nearer here. Marilla, what if she goes away?'

She said, 'If that was me, and the man I'd loved for twenty years had just come back into my life, a limpet would have nothing on me, I'd just be impossible to prise from Wanaka. She won't leave the Lake.' Then she added, smilingly, 'And what would you do if she did, Stephen?'

'Get out of here by chopper the moment the weather's favourable and chase her back to Wellington. They're bound to bring a chopper in later on, if the phone's cut, to see if we're holding out all right with supplies.'

'Then it's only a matter of a week or two, and anyway, the phone may be on again by night.'

They went out, collected Jane and Anne and Tony from working near Rufus, and went further up the hill near the homestead with them, while he moved on up the private road bluffs to the men.

Up here they found sheep under the overhang of the banks. Little steaming holes betrayed their whereabouts. Tony was sturdily built and in splendid condition and Steve had years of experience behind him. The girls too were surprisingly strong, considering their slender build. And this was their life, sheep, snow, the come-and-go of the seasons with all their hazards, the philosophy and acceptance of a high-country family.

Stephen whistled softly as he worked, tunes Marilla recognized as airs Elfreda would have played on the piano here. Looking at him, she realized he'd shed ten years since that conversation with Elfreda, frustrating and all as it had been.

By the time they all got back to the homestead, they were bone-weary, scratched, uncomfortably moist under their windcheaters. But hot baths or showers restored them. Rufus bore Tony off to a tub of steaming hot water immediately, and Marilla got both girls into one up to their necks, then said not to dress again, just to get into their warm ski-type pyjamas, snugly fitting round necks and ankles. They had bedsocks on, lambswool slippers, pure wool dressing-gowns.

While the men did the dishes Marilla mixed her junket into wholemeal and white flour, with its little bit of sugar, soda and salt sifted into it. She formed her dough into big round loaves, and put them on the bottom shelf of the great oven. Rufus had begun to protest, then conceded that her mind would be easier if she had some fresh bread on hand to eke out the diminishing supply of baker's bread in the freezer. As she said, soda bread took no longer than mixing a batch of scones.

They made it into the lounge in time for the newsbrief. It had been fairly widespread, the snow, but not nearly as disastrous as the October fall in Canterbury and North Otago in 1973, though stock losses in certain areas were to be expected. There were several districts without power, namely the Mackenzie country and the Lakes District. A further fall was expected, but not of the same density. Power would be restored as soon as humanly possible but further breaks could be expected. With the promptness of a stage cue, the Blue Canyon lights went out.

Stephen and Rufus went outside to swing the great kerosene lantern in the tower into position.

After that, they all got drowsy. There was something to be said for lamplight and firelight. Jane fell asleep on her uncle's knee, Anne on Marilla's. They rose, carried them along the carpeted passageway. The beds were turned down a little, so they pushed them down further, slipped the gowns off the little figures, tucked them in, looked at each other across the twin beds, smiled. Nothing was said. Nothing had to be. This was an affinity of spirit.

By the time Tony was ready for bed they all were. It would be another big day tomorrow.

But the second fall, as predicted, was lighter. It had obliterated the footsteps of yesterday, but wasn't deep, and the paths they had tramped out for the sheep to the sunnier faces were still discernible. But it would be a long day of feeding out.

Right at the end of it, Rufus, Stephen, the children and Marilla toiled up to a small plateau where a few sheep might need some supplementary stuff, and which couldn't be reached by tractor. While they were up there, wearing dark glasses, against the glare of the sun on the dazzling whiteness, Rufus, looking down, said, 'Look, the weight of snow from yesterday on the roof of your old hut, Steve, has been too much for the chimney. You'd notice we only use it for storing hay in now – look.'

The old chimney, built outside the hut, and which had been showing gaps for some time, had suddenly collapsed into a pile of rubble.

Rufus said, 'It doesn't matter, it held so little. The roof's still on. That'll keep the hay dry. We'll look at it as we go by, but no going inside, it may have weakened the roof-timbers. I'll have it demolished when we're over this bad patch.'

It was a sorry sight somehow. Even the old mantelpiece had fallen out with it, an old clock that had long since ceased to mark the hours, a kerosene lamp with its glass smashed. Suddenly Jane darted forward and said, 'What's that sticking to the back of the mantelpiece?'

She pulled at a letter that came away in her hands. It was filthy, had been chewed by silverfish, but was practically whole. She peered at the envelope. Her face changed. 'It's addressed to you, Steve, but there's no stamp on it. It just says: "Steve".' She flipped it over, said, 'Why, I don't think it's ever been opened.'

Stephen, vastly intrigued, tore it open, stared at another envelope inside it, and a pencilled note. The paper was yellow and the pencil very faint. But it was the other envelope he was staring at. It was stamped but not postmarked, and it was addressed in his own neat writing to ... Miss Elfreda Grant, at her Wellington address! He gave his head a little shake, said, 'But it can't be – It was—' he scanned the note. It was signed by one Barney who had worked on Blue Canyon at that time. It simply said: 'Dear Steve, sorry about this, mate, but as you went busting up to Wellington so soon after writing this letter to see your girl, I thought I'd better not post it *now*. I'm leaving for a job in Southland nearer home. You know you gave me this to post in Wanaka that night – well, I was given a few others. I put them in the post-box in a bunch. You could have knocked me down with a feather when I came across this in my pocket when I was packing. I hadn't worn my coat since, you see. Still, you'll have seen Elfreda long since and probably told her everything that was in the letter. Hope you didn't get into hot water for not writing – women set an awful lot of store by letters. I'll just leave it here for you. Best of luck, Barney.'

Stephen looked directly at Marilla, seeing she knew most about it. 'It's that letter I wrote Elfreda apologizing. I'd asked Barney to post it for me. Listen.' He read it out

– Barney's letter. The children, wide-eyed, were trying to imagine what it was all about. Elfreda, their beloved Frederica Moorcroft. They had a feeling they'd better not interrupt. If they did, for sure the grown-ups would send them off.

Stephen said, 'And of course I didn't come back. I couldn't face Blue Canyon without her. I worked my passage on a ship to Liverpool. It's been there all this time.' He looked at the children, smiled. 'Jane, Anne, Tony, I wanted to marry your Frederica all those years ago, but we quarrelled – my fault. So I wrote apologizing, and followed on the heels of my letter – as I thought – to see her and was told by someone rather nasty that she'd gone to Norfolk Island to dodge me.'

'Nasty like a witch?' breathed Anne.

'Witch-like is right,' said Stephen.

Jane said, eyes a-star, 'But it'll be all right now, won't it, because Marilla knows her. So does Guy. They'll give you her address.'

Rufus said hurriedly, 'It's as simple as that to children. But, girls, it was very good of Stephen to put us in the picture, so we mustn't ask him any more questions – I mean, about what he's going to do. Steve, I think—'

Steve was smiling broadly. 'Don't hush them up, Rufus. It's natural they want to know what I'm going to do. And it's more simple than you think. She's at this moment staying in Wanaka itself. No, no magic about that. She came down for a pony-club meeting in Canterbury, and thought she'd come on down here – may have wanted to visit old haunts, I don't know. But she did want to see Marilla. Not that Marilla got a chance to speak to her – she rang, you see, but I answered the phone.'

Jane clapped her hands to her mouth to check the words that were bursting out of her. Anne began jumping up and down. 'What did she say? What did she think?'

Stephen grinned. 'She wanted to know if I was married. I told her she was to stay where she was till she can get a helicopter to bring her in. I think she agreed.'

Rufus said, 'You *think*! What can you m—'

Stephen pulled a face. 'Right in the middle of it was when the line went.'

It was too much for Tony. He burst out laughing. 'What did you say, Steve? That must have been some moment!'

Jane said indignantly, 'It is *not* funny. It's terrible. It—'

Anne interrupted her. She had a sort of dreaming look. She looked up at Steve with her pixie-face. 'It will come right. She'll drop in from the skies. You could get married *here,* in the chapel, Mum and Dad were. Jane and I could be bridesmaids. We could wear long dresses and wreaths of flowers in our hair, and carry baskets of roses just like the little girls in her story. Just imagine ... us, bridesmaids to Frederica Moorcroft!'

'Jeepers!' said Tony in disgust. 'Listen to them. Girls! They've got on to clothes already. Besides, it's manners to wait till you're asked.'

Stephen looked down on them twinkling. 'I'm asking you here and now. She's not getting away from me a second time.' He flicked the tops of their heads affectionately. 'After all, if this letter had only been posted, I might have had some little girls like you by now. And perhaps sons, older.' His tone held infinite regret.

Jane caught the tone, Jane, who liked to pour oil on troubled waters, who wanted everyone to be happy. She looked up at him consideringly, said, 'I don't suppose you're so very old, really, Steve. I mean not *too* old. It would depend on Frederica, though, wouldn't it? Marilla, how old do ladies have to be before—'

Her uncle clapped his hand smartly over her mouth. 'Jane! You've already arranged his wedding for him, damned if I'll let you arrange his future family too. Now off! And when Elfreda gets here, you're not to speak a word about this to her. Marilla, I'll leave you here with Stephen. You may have things to discuss. After all, you've known Elfreda for years. Right, kids, scram!'

CHAPTER ELEVEN

MARILLA thought she would never forget the sunset that night. They finished earlier. The sky above them was a clear, soft azure blue. Over to the west was an arch of cloud, blown up from the mountains as if a nor'west wind was approaching across the Tasman instead of a southerly beating up from the Pole, for a change.

'Red sky at night, shepherd's delight,' said Rufus in her ear as she stood at the upstairs landing window, watching. She'd just put hotwater bottles in Stephen's bed and Rufus's. They could refill them later.

Rufus said, 'The thaw will set in tomorrow. The glass is rising. It's amazing how quickly it will go. Of all the southern lakes, Wanaka gets the most sunshine.'

She turned a little towards him. 'Rufus, do you think they'll send a helicopter in quite soon now to take Stephen and Guy and the others out?'

'I expect so. Of course Stephen's movements could depend upon your friend Elfreda. Before he goes he wants to see our furthest-out hut. Some have been erected since his day. He wants to see if they could be added to for accommodation for trampers. There's the possibility of this being used as access to a new ski-field. It could be less prone to avalanches than the one first thought of. Although this isn't part of a National Park, Dad's in favour of it. I think they'll send in for Steve to see the Park officials in Wanaka, and if he returns, maybe he'll bring his Elfreda in. They won't be parted so soon then. Imagine the kids . . . Steve'll be lucky if he gets any of her time at all then.'

'Rufus, that'll be just wonderful. It's good of you to think about having her here for an indefinite period. No wonder Blue Canyon's gained such a reputation for hospitality – if they're all like you.'

Rufus had a peculiar look on his face. He put on an act,

peered at her. 'Marilla, can this be you? Why, I do believe you've forgotten my first harsh reception of you.'

She started to laugh. 'I had. How funny. Yet at the time I could have boiled you in oil. That's why—' she came to a full stop.

He looked at her curiously. 'That's why you—?'

'Let that go. I'm always rushing into rash speech at the wrong moments. That's what got me into this. But, Rufus, I ought never to have lashed out at you as I did at that moment. I thought I'd learned a good deal of self-control in my years as a teacher, but I slipped badly, then.'

He said, 'But maybe you were upset about something yourself then. Just as I was all het-up because of all that had happened. Were you upset, Marilla? Was I, as you were to me, the last straw?'

She clasped her hands together nervously. 'You were – in a way. I'd – I'd *had* men just then, so I took it out on you. And in any case, most of what I was feeling was my own fault. I'd brought it on myself.' She stopped. Now was no time to go into that. Any moment someone might come racing upstairs. They weren't even in a room.

He seemed to notice her slight withdrawal, to terminate this conversation. He put out a hand to stop her moving away, drew her back to face the sunset again, slipped his arm about her shoulders.

'Marilla, tell me about that some time – when we get rid of some of this crowd. You said to Stephen, that time I came upon you, and waited because I didn't want to break up what seemed a very private conversation, that Elfreda hadn't let other people censure you. Well, whatever it was, don't be afraid I'll censure you either. Naturally you had a life of your own before you came here – and pressures in the city are sometimes tougher than up among the mountains. I just hope it didn't upset you too much, that's all. But I don't expect it was very much. You're a girl of high ideals, and might have worried over it too much.'

Marilla felt warmth flood her. She said, 'Oh, Rufus, thank you.'

She put a hand out. He took it in his. She could feel the callouses on his palms. She could also feel strength from him flowing into her. 'I – I do have something to tell you, Rufus. Maybe I've seemed a little secretive at times. You see I wasn't sure if you'd understand, or believe me.'

She turned her head a little so she could look up into the warm tawny eyes. She smiled a little. 'I've an idea you *would* believe me, now. I thought at first it was something you'd never understand. But – oh, Rufus, this is no time to be discussing this. I must see to the bread.'

She turned, but it brought her closer to him. He took her chin in his fingers, tilting it. 'I'm banking on that talk we're going to have, when we get time, for clearing up everything between us. I'm determined to dispel all those funny ideas you seem to harbour about believing in marriage but it not being for you, so I think we're quite justified in this . . .'

He kissed her lightly, but lingeringly.

They heard Tony's voice at the head of the stairs, 'Stone the crows!' it said. 'More love! It must be catching.'

They sprang apart and laughed. Tony was grinning from ear to ear. 'It's all right, I won't tell those clunky girls, cross my heart. Besides, I'd think this was a bit of all right if it means what I think it means.' They all laughed again.

'Uncle Rufus, I came up to see if you could possibly spare me some time on my telescope tonight. It's going to be clear. Only I know—'

'You know we're busy and tired. I appreciate that, Tony, and it would be in ideal conditions tonight. Thank your lucky stars, boy, that Marilla's just put me in a very good mood. I'll help her with her bread first, then we'll have a session up there in the end gable.'

The snow disappeared like magic in the hot November sun that succeeded the storm. Stephen was beginning to chafe a little under the knowledge that they had no way of communicating that they would like a chopper to come in to take him out. Marilla saw him climb way above the Lantern Hill house one night, and gaze through the cleft in the hills for a glimpse of the lake waters, no doubt thinking that the waters he could see were lapping against the shore where his Elfreda would pace each day, longing for him to come.

Late in the afternoon of the next day, Marilla, making girdle scones to eke out the bread, heard a great shout from outside. She had the three children at the kitchen table under her eagle eye, writing essays on the recent snowfall and comparing them with others, in years past.

They all rushed outside. Here were Rufus, Stephen and Guy, who'd been busy tightening some fencing near the creek, straining their eyes eastward and slightly south.

'Look,' said Rufus, as they joined the men, pointing, 'round the corner of the donkey track – see, we're having visitors. They've come right through from Fergussons' by the look of it. A man and a boy, I'd say. They've got bulging saddle-bags. Must be the Fergusson boys. Oldest and youngest, perhaps.'

They all set off, Marilla thanking her lucky stars she'd made such a huge batch of scones. The children outdistanced them, of course. Tony turned round, cupped his hands, shouted back to them, 'It's Edward Campbell. And it's not a boy, it's a woman. But not Fiona.'

'A woman!' Rufus was flabbergasted. 'That's the devil of a ride for a man, let alone a woman.'

Curiosity quickened their steps, but it was steep, this track, winding round the hill. The riders, sagging in their saddles, looked as if they couldn't coax an extra spurt out of their mounts.

All of a sudden Stephen, well back in the cavalcade, made a strange, incredulous sound. Then he passed them like a streak of lightning, but as he shot past Marilla he shouted, 'Don't you see? It's Elfreda!'

Guy said, 'It is, you know. She's a magnificent horse-woman, but – but this is astounding!'

Stephen had caught the children up and passed them.

In fact they'd stopped stock still with sheer surprise at his pace, then they turned and looked back uncertainly at the other party. Marilla said, 'Get them, for heaven's sake, Rufus. Let Stephen and Elfreda have this moment to themselves.'

The next instant they had to laugh. The three children must have guessed their intentions, and took off like greyhounds after Stephen.

Rufus said, 'Why try to stop them? In fact, I envy them. They won't be a bit embarrassed. They thoroughly enjoy love-scenes, as you know full well, Marilla.'

She saw her brother dart a quick, knowing glance at her and hastily looked away. Although they had checked, they stood watching, smiling. They knew the exact moment when Elfreda recognized the figure in the lead. She straightened in the saddle, dug her heels in, somehow got a little more speed out of her mount.

Edward Campbell, in the know about it, as he told them later, reined in.

Stephen was still ahead of the children when he reached her. The horse came to a willing stop, hung its head. Elfreda looked down, smiling. Stephen, having got there, seemed incapable of movement. Elfreda swung a stiff, breeched leg over the saddle, slid down, almost fell against him, and said, 'Well, if Mahomet won't come to the mountain, the mountain must come to Mahomet!'

She was seized then, held off from him a little so he could look hungrily at her, then she was caught to him and kissed most ruthlessly.

Marilla, tears slipping down her face, caught Rufus's hand. Then she said, 'Oh, Rufus, do something about those girls. Look at them, they're jumping up and down with glee!'

But Tony, who'd been level with the girls, suddenly recollected himself and his year or two's superiority. He turned, seized each girl by the scruff of the neck, and marched them, protesting loudly, back to the group.

Edward Campbell rode past the couple, laughing, but not looking, and on to them. He said, dismounting, 'I'm pretty stiff myself and I reckon Frederica ought to be. Oh, listen – I'm as bad as my own children. Robert and Elspeth are as much fans of hers as ever my nieces and nephews were. I was delighted to meet her again when I called to see Brigid Granville yesterday. I told them the County Engineer had talked me into riding here to give them an idea of the changed situation from this end. Blest if Elfreda didn't announce she was coming with me. It wasn't a case of asking if she could come. I could remember Steve teaching her to ride, so asked very cautiously had she kept it up. Brigid burst out laughing and put me in the picture. She put me wise about other things too' – he turned and surveyed the couple with a twinkle – 'and I found myself doing it.'

Marilla knew that Edward Campbell, though he owned Belle Knowes Station, a remote one served only by launch, was a roading engineer who'd had to return to farming when his older brother had been killed.

They discovered that meanwhile the two figures had separated, were walking towards them, Stephen leading the horse, Elfreda holding Stephen's hand.

The usual chaffing things were said when the greetings were over, then they began walking down to the homestead. Marilla was overflowing with happiness for Elfreda and Stephen, but thought, somewhat despairingly, that the house-party just grew bigger and bigger.

Elfreda changed into a very dashing trouser-suit after a hot bath and didn't complain of as much stiffness as Edward did. Guy kept looking at her the way the ugly duckling's mother must have kept looking at the alabaster beauty of her swan.

After dinner Stephen and Elfreda disappeared. Rufus had lit the fire in his mother's sitting-room for them. He had banished them there, when he'd finally succeeded in prising Jane and Anne away from her. They'd wanted to go over every book with her.

The two girls went to bed almost perfectly happy. True perfection would have been to have been able to tell their father and mother about it, especially that they'd been asked to be bridesmaids.

All Marilla seemed to do for the next few days was to make enormous and very plain meals and supervise lessons. Elfreda pitched in with keeping the house tidy, though Marilla tried to free her as much as possible from that so she could catch up on some of the wasted hours of her life and spend them with Stephen. What did it matter if Green Gables lacked a bit of spit and polish? They had all come through a time of emergency, even danger, without lasting harm, and a wrong of twenty years ago had been righted.

Edward Campbell's report lightened their hearts. A new road could be bulldozed in, he thought, much more easily than at first expected. The landslip had also swept away what might have been a major bar to that, if a road there had been attempted when the first one had been put through. Though it would take time to bridge the river, the crossing was so narrow at the most strategic point that they could be given a boat-crossing, fixed to pulleys, if they built a pontoon, fixed to a very convenient tree this side.

He would get them to put a standard the other side, and another pontoon, coming from the Matukituki valley side. Long before Christmas they'd be able to ferry themselves across and take off for Wanaka whenever necessary.

Elfreda, in a private conference with Marilla, offered to see Rufus and explain that she was really Eleanor St. John. Marilla shrank visibly. She begged her not to. 'I can't stand the thought of it with so many people in the house.' Elfreda agreed; she'd had so much interference in her own affairs, she wouldn't meddle now. And she thought Rufus's natural resentment at being made such a fool of would be much less if fewer people – in fact only his men – were there at the time. It was going to be dicey.

Stephen and Elfreda's companionship was lovely to behold. She even went right up to the huts with him and his men, sleeping rough, and enjoying every moment.

She'd said, 'I'm so glad we're to be married in the chapel here. I couldn't bear it back home, with the aunts disapproving. When I think—'

Stephen had looked thoughtful. 'Elfreda, we are going to invite them to the wedding. They can stay in Wanaka and we'll fly them in by helicopter if necessary. Poor, lonely selfish old things. I don't think bitterness should be kept up. They won't be allowed to interfere, I promise you, but I think you'd be happier if we didn't cut them out altogether.'

Elfreda looked radiant. 'Oh, Stephen, I love you more than ever. It was only that I wasn't going to run any chance of you being hurt again. I mustn't harbour any bitterness, either. I expect it wasn't the easiest, taking a brother's child into a spinster household, and they looked after me well enough, according to their lights.'

There came the day when the phone rang to announce the line was restored; shortly after they had power again. They got word that Stephen's Wanaka contacts wanted to see him, and the National Parks Board. He rang his Department, reported what he thought about eventual access through Blue Canyon, and was able, after his next ring, to report gleefully to Rufus that this could easily mean the erection of the bridge would get higher priority than expected. Things moved quickly, and soon they were facing their last night in Blue Canyon, all together. Edward Campbell was going out with them. The horses could be returned by Rufus's men any time. The Fergussons weren't needing them.

They had an hilarious night, making it an engagement party for Elfreda and Stephen. It was quite late when they broke it up. Marilla decided that however late, she'd add a page or two to that gigantic letter for her parents, that would go out with the others, in the mailbag. She felt almost content. When the toast had been drunk to the engaged couple, Rufus had proposed another, 'To Marilla, who has kept the home fires burning,' and it had been drunk very heartily. It augured well for her moment of revelation.

Just as she turned her blankets down, there came a discreet tap on the French windows that opened on to the courtyard of the little cottage.

For a moment she felt scared, then told herself not to be so stupid. There was no one but themselves in their isolated world. It came again, and a whisper said, 'Marilla, let me in, it's Guy.'

She unlatched the window very quietly. He was in dressing-gown and pyjamas. She drew him in quickly. 'Guy, it may be the last month of spring, but we've still a lot of snow on the tops. You'll catch your death!'

'Oh, shucks. You're as bad as Mum. I wanted a word with you. There's never been a chance all day – it's like living in an institution, just milling crowds of people all the time. Look, Sis, you and Rufus seem to be on a very friendly footing, to put it mildly, so isn't it time you spilled the beans to him? And tell me, what am I to tell Mother? I'll have to ring her from Wanaka to say where I am, and the Inquisition will have nothing on her – you know that. I could tell she was just about dying of curiosity when I spoke to her on the phone that night, but she daren't say a word, poor lamb, that might trip me up in the hearing of the others, when I was calling her Aunt Helena all the time! Really, what parents go through! So do tell Rufus as soon as you can. Pick the right moment, though, and don't be stupid enough to blow your top if he blows his. He's entitled to. You've made a fool of him, but he's so fond of you, he'll forgive you – eventually.'

Oh dear, he was doing nothing for her confidence. She said, 'He told me the other day he thought I was hiding something. I admitted I was, and that I'd tell him the truth when we weren't so busy and could get a moment to ourselves. I was just going to start baking bread. He's nowhere near the truth, of course. He thinks I'm running away from an unhappy love affair. Could anything be further from the facts?'

The next moment she'd clutched him. 'Guy, you idiot ... don't guffaw out loud like that! They'll hear you upstairs. Though I guess they'll be sound asleep.'

His voice became a thread of sound. 'They'd never know what woke them. I'll guffaw silently from now on. A second James Bond was lost in me.'

She whispered witheringly, 'I don't recall James Bond being secretive about his affairs. Blatant is more the word. Now listen, Guy. Tell Mother all is well, that I'm about to confess to Rufus, and as by now he thinks I'd make a good governess for his sister's children, and having me here would get him out of the scrape he's in with his sister, I'm sure he'll believe I didn't come up here aware of a deep-laid plot between Brigid and Diana and his mother.'

Guy heaved a sigh. 'Marilla, the first thing Mother's going to ask is: "Has she fallen for this Rufus?" '

Marilla clutched him again. They were sitting on the edge of her bed. 'Guy, I'll murder you if you as much as hint that I—' she came to a dead stop.

Guy surveyed her with an enormous grin, whispered, 'Let me finish it for you. If I as much as hint that you *have* fallen for him.' Then he relented. 'All right, I won't. If you like I'll say, "Good heavens, no, the chaps engaged to a girl in Wanaka." That better?'

'Guy!'

He said, 'Stop clutching me. I'll be black and blue.'

She said, 'It's less noisy than groaning. Guy, you aren't to fool about with this. That would only make it more complicated when—' she came to another full stop.

Guy was shaking. He put his arm round her and hugged her. 'It's all right, muggins, I've got eyes in my head. You were going to say it would trip you up when you *are* able to tell Mother all, and she has to receive Rufus into the bosom of the family. Now, don't tell me I'm going too fast, it's as plain as a pikestaff. You should hear the men's views on it! I think it's ideal. But I won't jump the gun, nor will I overplay my hand. After all, it's not like having to talk to Mother face to face. It'll be on long distance and you know how thrifty she is. I'll say cautiously that there could be an attraction there, but I'm not sure. That we'd better give them time. Much better than a too-vigorous denial, I think.'

'So do I,' breathed Marilla fervently, vastly relieved. They chatted on, glad to have the chance of uninhibited, private talk. Then Marilla quietly let him out and Guy stepped outside. Guy bent down, caught hold of his sister, gave her a close hug, said, 'I'm sure everything will turn out right, Rilla.' He kissed her and fled.

They woke to a glorious day, scarcely a cloud in the sky. The peaks stood out in sharp silver relief against the blueness. What wonderful things these small, whirring birds of the sky were. The lifeboats of the air, they called them in these regions, because of the lives they had saved, winching injured climbers out of the depths into which they had fallen.

They wasted no time, because they had several other errands to do today. It was wonderful to see such a stack of bread, fruit, vegetables, newspapers, magazines and mail, lovely, lovely mail. Marilla had to confess that cooking for a mere eight would be nothing after what she'd been through.

Nevertheless she felt very flat when they had gone. And she knew why. What was the matter with Rufus? He was taciturn to the point of being rude.

Gone was all the camaraderie of the past weeks, the feeling of growing intimacy, the moment the helicopter left. Till then, he'd been, she thought, his usual self. He wasn't even meeting her eyes.

It was a case of: 'Well, they're gone, let's get cracking,' to the men, then, to Marilla, 'We'll be working further away today. I'll pack a haversack.'

As she said, 'I'll get you some sandwiches,' he said, 'No, no, we don't want any fuss. Those cold pasties'll do, and some bread and cheese and flasks. But I'll get them. I want those children into the schoolroom catching up on things as soon as possible. Most of the morning's gone now. With us not in for lunch, that's going to give you more time for lessons. Mind, they're only to take half an hour for theirs.'

Marilla, hurt, said, 'I've managed to keep fairly well to date with their sets. But when they had to go out on the hill, they lost a bit, but we'll easily catch up now. Then I couldn't—'

'Of course you couldn't – then. Didn't expect it. I'm just pointing out they've got to get their noses right down today, not getting at you. Kids, straight in, and get your things out. If you postpone their lunch till one-thirty, they might get a bit of work done before that. They gorged themselves at snack-time, so it won't hurt. And I expect them to really have something to show by four.'

Marilla said, 'Very sensible. Right, children, into the cottage.'

As they went out of the door she turned a little uncertainly towards him. He said, 'Marilla, I've told you I'll put this up myself. I think they'll take a bit of settling down after the excitement of the chopper. I'd rather you were with them.'

Stung, she said, 'I merely thought it might have been a matter of priorities. That if you've a big, but short, day ahead, it might help if I put up the pasties and sliced the bread, while you're getting the men organized. The children will settle all right. They know what I'm like if they don't. Discipline has never been a problem with me.'

'I thought that at first, too. Now I'm wondering.'

'Wondering? What on earth can you mean? Wondering what?'

His eyes met hers. She'd never imagined those red-brown eyes could look so cold. Fiery, yes. Tempery, yes, but not cold.

'Wondering if, after all, you mightn't be a little lax.'

Marilla's mouth fell open. Then she managed, 'I can't even begin to imagine what you mean.'

When he didn't reply, but opened the fridge to get the cheese, she added, 'Unless you mean they call me Marilla instead of Miss Sinjin. But at the time I let them, I didn't expect to be here more than two nights.'

'That wasn't what I meant,' he said.

Marilla brought her hand down smack on the table-top. 'Then you just explain yourself! I've no use for innu-endoes and barbed remarks. I like straight speaking. What's gone wrong?'

He snorted. 'You don't like innuendoes? You prefer straight speaking – oh, bosh, don't give me that. Not any more. I've been really disillusioned in you.' He actually clenched his fists. 'You've been living a lie all this time.'

She swallowed. What a moment for it to happen! His men would be looking for him any moment. She said, 'Rufus, we were going to have a talk, remember? I said I'd something to tell you. In fact, it was a confession – about this. I – I thought we'd become such – such pals that it mightn't now make the difference it might have made, had you known earlier. I know you thought it was something different, but—'

'I certainly did think it was something different. Pals, yes, we *were* pals. I thought you'd fallen for someone married, and, being you, as I thought you were then, had cut and run. But I didn't think of anything like this. You said you didn't want marriage, but—'

At that moment the most appalling din broke out in the direction of the cottage. Flying footsteps sounded along the concrete lead-in, and through the open door-way Anne came flying, full of rage, tears spilling down her cheeks, the little striped top over her jeans a sorry mess of red ink.

'Look what he's done! Look!'

Tony rushed in behind her, guilt written all over an appalled countenance. 'Marilla, I didn't mean it. Truly. It was an accident.'

Jane fell in the door, trying to gasp out an explanation.

Rufus roared, 'Jane! Had *you* anything to do with this?'

'No, but it was only an—'

'Then get back to the schoolroom! I want you kids settled down in five minutes flat. By the look of this mess, there'll be more spilt back there.' He tossed her the dish-cloth. 'Mop it up with that and throw it into the garden.

Then get out the books and start your own. Scram!'

Jane vanished.

Rufus said in icy tones, 'How did it happen, Tony?'

He looked ashamed. 'Well, I – I picked up a rubber and flicked it across at her from the tip of my ruler and it hit the bottle of ink. I hadn't realized it had the top off. I'm sorry.'

Marilla was surprised to see colour rush up into Anne's face. Then she gulped and said, 'It wasn't all his fault. I – I was being tantalizing. I'd hidden his pencil-sharpener.'

Marilla could have hugged her. The spunky little kid, owning up to that! And Tony hadn't told on her. Before Rufus could get a word out she said, 'Thank you, Anne. You didn't let him take all the blame. It's a very minor matter after all. Ink's been spilled before. Pity it's so hard to get out, that's all. Rufus, the schoolroom behaviour is *my* province, *I'll* see to it. Tony, back to the schoolroom and sharpen all the pencils. Where did you put the sharpener, Anne?'

She fished in her pocket and held it out to her brother. Marilla took hold of her striped top. 'I'll stretch the neck as I take it off, but close your eyes, we don't want red ink on your face.' She peeled it off, said, 'Oh, it's got your vest too.' Off it came. 'Now into your room and get something else on, and straight back to the schoolroom through the french windows of my room. Waste no time.'

'No,' said Anne meekly, disappearing with the tadpole-like agility of one who, often, has found it better not to wait upon the order of her going, when in the presence of wrathful grown-ups.

Marilla seized a basin, grabbed a jug of milk from the fridge, poured it over the two garments, said sarcastically, 'I do trust you don't think I'm wasting time, but I imagine your sister would rather have this ink stain out than save five minutes in the schoolroom. I find you utterly and completely inconsistent – no conscience at all about working them outside in the snow, then using steamroller tactics to get them on lessons about sixty seconds after we've got rid of our visitors.'

Rufus thrust the flask he'd filled into the bag with such violence they'd be lucky if they had a hot drink at all. 'Imagine *you* telling *me* I'm inconsistent! That's a laugh. You're about the most contradictory female it's ever been my misfortune to meet. I could have stacked my all on your integrity – almost did, in fact. So if you have any ideas about disarming me, Marilla, you can give them up right now. Don't keep on practising your wiles on me. I've seen through them.'

He'd seen through them. In the midst of her fury Marilla found herself wondering how he'd found out. Perhaps Stephen had let something slip. Or Elfreda, in a well-meant endeavour at trying to temper the wind to the shorn lamb. Or perhaps it had suddenly added up ... Elfreda's mention of staying with Brigid Granville, for instance.

At that moment her eyes fell on the jug she'd just used. 'Hell and damnation!' she said in a tone of ultimate rage. 'That wasn't milk, it was cream! Now look what you've made me do! I'll have to get grease out now as well as ink. Ohh!' She actually gritted her teeth.

Unforgivably, Rufus laughed. 'I wish you well of your job,' he said, flung the bag over his shoulder and departed.

Marilla stamped her foot, was just about to stamp the other when she pulled herself together. She might get caught out by one of the children, and what a letdown for them that would be, seeing an adult in a childish paddy. She let her fury expend itself in furiously rubbing almost boiling water through the garments to rid them of the cream, then soaking them in milk. There'd be no cream for the apple-pie tonight, and serve Rufus right!

When she entered the schoolroom, three heads were bent over their separate desks, their sets of lessons spread out before them, and much work had been done. She busied herself with some papers for a while till her anger, if not vanquished, was at least subdued.

She worked herself and the children at such a pace, the scene receded a little from her mind. She was setting some tests when lunchtime arrived. She looked up. 'I want to finish these. Would you go and set the table? Quickly and without quarrelling. If your uncle should come in at two, I want him to find us back here. We'll just have soup and a slice each of that cold bacon-and-egg pie. Okay?'

'Wilco,' said Tony, as usual. The three of them stood up, shuffling their papers to neatness. Suddenly Anne slipped behind Marilla's chair, put her arms round her neck, gave her a swift kiss on the cheek, joined the others at the door.

Jane gave her her wide sweet smile. Tony cleared his throat. 'Marilla,' he said, 'thanks for saving us from the wrath that seemed about to come.'

Marilla was horrified to find a rush of tears start to her eyes. The children stared, fascinated. Anne said quickly, 'Marilla, don't worry about Uncle Rufus. He's hardly ever mad, and he never stays that way. He *was* grumpy this morning, wasn't he? But he'll be all right tonight.'

Tony nodded sagely, 'It's been a bit much. I thought he was taking it a bit too cheerfully – I mean, a hill disappearing and the road washed out, then the snow, but we thought—'

Marilla knew by experience that if children stopped, having had second thoughts, it was wiser not to prompt them, but she couldn't help herself. 'You thought—?'

Tony went red. 'We thought he didn't care because he liked having you here and thought the longer we were cut off, the longer you'd have to stay. Marilla, we've been dying to ask you. You *will* stay on to teach us, won't you?'

She said slowly, 'That's something I've got to talk out with your uncle, Tony. I can't make a decision yet. Now you must get cracking.'

'Too right,' said Jane. 'We'll be models. Then Uncle Rufus will be bound to want you to stay.' They vanished.

Marilla sat still, thinking. It was nothing to do with her standard of teaching. It was just that her deception had bitten deeply into Rufus. He'd probably read all sorts of wrong motives into it, might have thought she'd enjoyed making a fool of him.

171

Tonight, when they had their showdown, or understanding, which ever it turned out, she must control her temper, her resentment of what he'd said this morning, and make an effort to get him to see how she'd felt, labelled a husband-hunter, when nothing could have been more remote from the truth. That she was running away from a surplus of would-be husbands!

If the men sat on for television, she'd say straight out, 'Rufus, may I see you in the schoolroom, please, about this next set of lessons?' What a relief it would be to confess the lot, to be candid for once. And it just could be that he'd ring his sister, and Diana might be able to convince him she hadn't been in the plot. Although, looking at it in the light of Rufus's attitude this morning, it was doubtful that he'd want her to stay on.

At the thought of leaving these children, Marilla knew a stab of regret like a physical pain. Once children came into your heart as these ones did, the loss of them could be unbearable.

The youngsters worked like Trojans, behaved like angels – oh, dear, her mind just naturally fell into clichés today, she was so tired. She just hoped she would be more eloquent tonight. She gave them their freedom at four and out into the glorious sunshine they ran, all fears forgotten. In response to their urging, she went out to play a game of Tag with them. The exercise loosened her tensions.

When she came in she decided she was far too hot in her slacks, had a shower after she popped the dinner in, and, perversely, decided she would still wear the dress she'd meant to wear tonight when she had so joyously planned that would be the ideal time for their talk when she would tell him her real identity. She'd waited one day too long, that was all.

She could slip a blue floral smock-top she had, with a deep blue yoke in dacron, over the dress. It would look just like a plain white skirt then, not too flossy for a dinner in a farm kitchen.

But when she got Rufus out to the schoolroom, she'd

have slipped the smock off, and the consciousness she was looking her best, might give her the confidence she sadly needed. As long as he didn't think it another wile! Oh, to the devil with that!

Clothes did do something for you. This, a summer frock, made her feel lighter-hearted. It was very simply cut, yet had been a wild extravagance in price. It had a high round neck with a ruffle round it. The short sleeves had the same ruffled edging that almost looked like a soft clipped wool, but was some synthetic material. It was slenderly cut, with no waistline, and was short enough to show her beautiful legs to fullest advantage. She pinned the sapphire brooch Granny Stewart had left her at one shoulder.

She wasn't sure what her motives were. Possibly she wanted to show Rufus Sinclair she wasn't the sort of girl who *needed* to go husband-hunting. On went the blue smock, hiding all this. She combed her luxuriant red hair into a style, catching it high on her head, and letting the curling ends fall to her shoulders. She pinned a pearl clasp in it to hold it firmly.

Now to the dinner, then to the showdown.

CHAPTER TWELVE

THE dinner was ready to dish by the time the men came in. She'd taken extra pains with the table. The poppies, saved before the storm, were lasting, a splash of colour amidst the blue dishes. Buck looked at Marilla and gave a wolf-whistle. 'You should always wear your hair like that, it's really something.'

She laughed easily enough. 'Haven't had time to breathe lately, much less set my hair. I've just been brushing it out and tying it back. Thought I'd better start preparing myself to get back to civilization soon. Having the helicopter in today made me realize it won't be long now before the emergency is over. Even if Donal won't dare come in till you've got the pulley-boat going, I daresay when he's a little stronger, Diana will bring him down to the crib at Wanaka, and have the children flown out to her there. And I'd be able to get out on the same flight.'

Buck started to make a surprised and vigorous objection, but Rufus, scrubbing up, said, 'Fair enough. Being marooned loses its novelty after a while, of course, especially when the company departs. I might ring Di tonight and find out just how Donal is doing. I could propose just that. I did say to the 'copter pilot that I might need him in some time before too long to fly you out, Marilla, but I hadn't thought about letting the children go in to Wanaka. In fact, Brigid Granville would have them till Di and Donal can get down.'

Marilla saw Evan, Buck, and Coll all look at her most uncertainly, then at each other. She managed a very unconcerned look. Rufus, from the scullery, his face half buried in the towel, said, 'Where are the kids? Watching Daniel Boone or something?'

Marilla's voice was deceptively casual. 'No, they're in the lounge, certainly, but they're doing some extra work.

Catching up, like you suggested.'

Rufus's voice was sharp. 'Heavens, they've not been at it all day, have they, missing all the sunshine?'

'Of course not. I kept them to the routine you suggested – half an hour for lunch, and lessons till four. Then we all played games, they did their chores outside, then went up Rainbow Valley to see if the bells were still chiming and to have a swing.'

She saw the men exchange another look; they were surmising a quarrel. Marilla called the children in to the meal-table. The children were unnaturally polite to each other and to the grown-ups. It was only policy when their elders were behaving like this. Evan, Buck, Coll, kept the conversation going nicely.

Suddenly Marilla got a kick on the leg. She looked surprised; she thought it had come from Buck. The next moment, looking at Coll and Evan, who'd presumably been meant to receive that signal, he said, 'Don't forget, chaps, we'll work out that trip tonight. Rufe, we'll just go across to our own sitting-room. Lindsay and Boyd want us to work it out for them. Way down Fiordland, in from Te Anau. We said we'd have it roughed out for them and let them have it, the first time we get the 'copter in to fly us out to Wanaka for a day off.'

'Fine,' said Rufus. 'That suits me.'

Marilla felt her heart give a funny little lurch. Did he want her on his own to tell her what he really thought? She'd have to try to get in first. Could he have arranged it with Buck to get the others out of the way?

No doubt he'd send the children off soon too. In which she was wrong. They'd gone scampering through the lounge and turned the TV on. As she came into the room, beautifully firelit and with just the big standard lamp on over the couch where the three children were sitting, he said from his chair, 'You can stay up a bit longer tonight, kids. You deserve it, the way you've worked.'

They beamed on him. Their uncle was himself again, it seemed.

Marilla had other ideas about that. He wanted to keep

the children there as a barrier against discussion. Well, he was in for a shock! Suppose it was midnight, he was going to listen to her. She took a seat as far distant as possible from him, yet with the screen still in view.

While the ads were on, Anne bounced up. 'Marilla, we've not seen you in that dress before. Do let's have a look at it. Take your smock off.'

'Girls,' said Tony, 'are always talking about clothes; or love.'

The girls ignored him. 'Jehosaphat,' said Jane, 'that's gorgeous! Let me touch that fur round the neck. Oh, it's not fur ... what is it?'

'Something synthetic. I like it myself. It makes you feel luxurious, yet it's not warm like fur, or tickly.'

'I like that brooch,' said Anne. 'It's a good one, isn't it?'

'Yes, poppet. It belonged to my granny. Well, not mine really, Guy's granny. A sort of step-grandmother.'

Rufus looked across and said, with a hint of irony, 'Oh, of course. The relationship between you and Guy is very close, isn't it?'

Well, she could expect him to be wild about Guy having carried on the pretence.

Rufus said, 'What's on next, Tony? Did you hear the programme?'

'No, we missed it, for now, I mean. We know what's on later. It sounded like some documentary. We just got the tail-end of the announcement.'

'Well, if it's any good you can watch it. If not, we'll turn it off and I'll give you a game of Scrabble.'

Benjamin Lemaud came on, began an introduction. Marilla was delighted. It would serve to illustrate to Rufus later exactly how she'd got caught up in this thing. She'd thought that particular roving commission was over, though. Oh, evidently it was something different.

'We're going to have a panel discussion later on, with the talking point marriage breakdown.' He gave the names of the panel, then paused, added, '... and the Reverend Angus St. John of St. Crispin's, and for that reason we are repeating a programme done some weeks ago,

176

which featured his daughter's views on marriage . . .'

Marilla gave a strangled gasp. Then to her amazement Rufus said, 'Good lord, I wonder if it'll be Eleanor St. John?'

Marilla felt the blood positively drumming in her ears. She vaguely heard Tony say, 'Who's she?' but she was staring in fascinated horror at the screen, and the next moment was watching Benjamin Lemaud come along the line of girls, microphone in hand, then pause . . . Now she was watching herself. She heard Rufus gasp, say, 'Why, that's—' there was a cry of recognition in chorus from the children, then everybody lapsed into surprised and listening silence, and Benjamin Lemaud's voice came in clearly, 'Now I just hope *you* are going to say something in *praise* of men, something *good* for marriage . . .'

Utterly dismayed, Marilla saw her screen image fling back the hair from her shoulders, say, laughingly, 'Here it comes, pals! Suppose you tear me to pieces afterwards, I'm going to be courageously honest and say I think most women have a wonderful life . . . it's all theirs . . .'

Nobody spoke. Benjamin kept calling her Marilla. She said her pieces about her parents . . . 'Even when they're flaming mad with each other – you still have the feeling they'd rather be that way with each other than insipidly polite with other people.'

Marilla felt her nerve going. In a moment or two, her voice on that soundtrack was going to utter that bit about the ideal life, the high-country sheep station beyond the foothills, and she could do nothing to stop it . . . the fateful words were said, Marilla's cheeks burned. She could not look at Rufus. Before she finished, the screen began to flicker, lines flashed madly across it. Marilla prayed madly that every valve in the set would blow up before she went on describing her heart's desire . . . oh, how could she have been so stupid? Tony and Rufus flew across the carpet, began twiddling things frantically Then the whole screen went blank, music began to play, the clock showed up and a voice apologized for the break in the network transmission. It would resume shortly.

'Thank goodness,' said Tony fervently. 'I was scared it was a local breakdown, and that only some viewers, us, would miss the next bit and the rest of the country'd get the lot and we'd only have the panel at the end. Gosh, Marilla, you're beaut on telly. Why didn't you tell us you'd been on a programme?'

She found her hands were shaking, so she clasped them together. She was awaiting Rufus's reaction. But he said nothing, so she said in a wobbly voice, 'Because I – I – I – because I didn't enjoy it much. Because afterwards—'

Rufus came out of his trance and demanded of her, '*Why* did you say your name was Sinjin? Why? Just tell me why?'

How could she explain it, in front of the children? She said quickly, 'Well, some people do call it Sinjin. Haven't you ever heard it pronounced that way? It's like your own name – Sinclair. That was originally St. Clair. You must know that.'

'But you gave it to Lemaud as St. John. Well, never mind why you did it, because I can understand, now, why you didn't let on later.'

Marilla's eyes went glassy. But he knew. He'd said, just this morning, he'd found out she was living a lie. What *could* he mean?

He said, and all anger was gone from his tone, 'It was because I asked you to take that letter to your sister, wasn't it? To Eleanor? You dared not say she was your sister. Of course you couldn't. Heavens – the things I said!' He looked at her sharply and she could almost see the wheels going round in his head. 'I get the whole thing now. You were here on holiday and your sister asked you to look this place over. Then I bawled you out and you decided it was no place for her. So when I asked your name, you said Sinjin. Tell me, Marilla, was I mistaken about Eleanor too? You took me for Donal, didn't you? Did Eleanor *not* know there was a bachelor owner up here, either? I mean, *was* she the victim of the match-makers too, all along? As I think you tried to tell me that night, only I wouldn't listen. If so, I apologize to

Eleanor.' A thought struck him. 'But she'll know *you're* here. I mean, your mother rang.'

He still hadn't got it. She waved an agitated hand, 'Rufus, what are you talking about?'

He blinked. 'What do you think I'm talking about?'

Tony said, in a grown-up tone, to his sisters, 'They've got their blinking wires crossed.'

His uncle said, 'Be quiet! Marilla, what—'

She said, 'Well, if you don't know, what on earth were you so furious about this morning? Why are you packing me off from here as soon as you can? No ... don't answer that yet, it'll only confuse the issue. Rufus, there isn't a sister Eleanor. *I'm* Eleanor. I'm Eleanor Marilla St. John. I was so embarrassed by that whole programme and the effect it had on my life that I applied as Eleanor M. None of this would have happened if Elfreda hadn't run into her old friend Brigid that day in Wellington. I wanted to get away because of that programme.

'I got pestered and pestered by men – some nice, some cranks, one even frightening. So I cut and run. It was dreadful. I applied for this post and came here on holiday, couldn't resist coming up to see what the place was like – and you were in that awful temper. I decided if Donal MacGillivray was like that I didn't want to teach his children. So I dared not say St. John, though I almost did. Then everything happened. For Guy to land here was the worst possible luck. Look, Tony, turn that thing off. I can't go on talking against that music. I don't want to see the rest of that programme, even if they do get it going again.'

'Never in your life,' said Rufus. 'I only hope they get it on soon. I'm intensely interested in your views on marriage. I'm trying to decide which is the real you, the one on the screen, or the one who kept proclaiming to me that marriage wasn't for her.'

Then Marilla lost her temper. Her cheeks flew the banners of rage, her hair, springing from its widow's peak, looked like an angry crest. She even felt a prickling at the nape of her neck ... hackles rising!

She clenched her hands, which were no longer shaking. 'Which is the real me? The one on the screen, of course. That was before I met you, when I could be perfectly natural, when I didn't have to watch every word. Of course I downed marriage to you. How else could I talk to a man who'd be bound to find out some day that I was Eleanor St. John, Eleanor, the husband-hunter! Who said he'd *never* believe she hadn't conspired with his sister and mother! I'd never heard of your mother, didn't know there *was* a bachelor up here. Believe me, if I'd known there was, you wouldn't have caught as much as a glimpse of me. I was running *away* from men, not *after* them. *They* all thought I was dying for a husband too, not that I was merely expressing my idealistic views on marriage and where I'd like best to live. One of them even smashed my granny's vase, when I wouldn't marry him. Of *course* I said to you marriage wasn't for me!'

Rufus said quietly, 'But that isn't all, I'm afraid. There's something else I must discuss with you later, something that will take more explaining than all that schemozzle. He said to the children: 'Sorry about this. No doubt Marilla and I will get it all sorted out in time.'

Three serious faces stared at him, then Tony said, 'Here we go, it's coming on again. Now for Pete's sake nobody talk while it's on.'

The apology was repeated, then Benjamin Lemaud's last sentence was recapped. It went smoothly on, with Marilla reiterating that she'd like to live in the high country. The children's faces lost their tenseness. Anne turned her face to Marilla's. 'And now you're here in the high country,' she whispered.

At last, mercifully, her part was over and Benjamin said, 'And now for our panel.'

Rufus shot to his feet to switch off, eager to get on with the discussion, but Marilla let out a protesting cry, 'No, *please*! Oh, let me see my father!'

Rufus stopped half-way across the hearthrug. Tony waved him back.

The Reverend Angus was the last to be introduced.

The others had all been asked for their occupations, their marital status, for the size of their families and their approximate ages.

Marilla didn't know that at the sight of her father, so dear, the comforter and protector of her early years, the tears began falling down her cheeks. Nor did anyone else, then. They were all too intent on the screen. Angus St. John said, 'My elder daughter you have just seen. I have a stepson, some years older, Guy Stewart, with a Government Department, and a younger twin son and daughter, Kit and Fiona, in their first year at Varsity.'

There was an indescribable sound from Rufus and a bound across the room, and a television set was switched off. He swung round. 'We've heard all we want to hear,' he said, and crossed to Marilla's chair.

She got to her feet, braced herself a little. He took her by the shoulders and shook her. He almost shouted it. 'Guy's your father's stepson? Stepson ... then that makes him your ...'

'My brother. My half-brother really. Look, Rufus, I'm in a whirl. I thought this was what you'd found out. That you'd found out I was Eleanor, that Guy was my brother ... that I'd made a right fool of you. Oh, we *were* awful, Guy calling my poor bewildered Mother Aunt Helena – oh, she knew from Elfreda I hadn't let on who I was, but—'

He shook his head as if to clear it. 'No, no. Look, when he first arrived, I was a bit jealous of him as an old boyfriend of yours, walking with him in the moonlight and all that. Then I cheered up, thought I could out-rival him. Okay, that sounds vain, I don't care if it does. I thought if he could leave you for three years, it served him right if someone else got you. I don't care, do you hear? Don't care about a damned thing, as long as he's your brother. But last night – I'll never forget last night—' he stopped abruptly, suddenly conscious of three rapt faces on the couch. They'd frozen into absolute stillness, terrified he might order them from the room and they'd miss the fun.

Marilla had forgotten them. Awareness was breaking over her in a mad, glad tide. She said clearly, 'Last night, you heard Guy come to my room? Is that it?'

The tawny eyes looked into the clear grey ones. 'Yes. The longest three-quarters of an hour of my life. And the most hideous.'

Marilla put up an impatient hand and dashed away her tears.

'Oh, Rufus, Rufus – why, I've never even been in love till now—' She suddenly became aware of their audience.

Jane came to life, her blue eyes sparkling. 'Oh, don't stop *now*!' she implored.

Anne collapsed, her wide gamin grin breaking into laughter. 'He said once we'd never be round when he proposed to a girl. He was wrong, wasn't he?' She paused and a look of incredible delight overspread her face. 'Jane! I reckon we're going to be bridesmaids ... *twice*!'

Her uncle started to laugh. 'Never in my whole life have I imagined I'd be in a situation like this. And what makes you think I'm about to propose?'

They looked anxious, all three. Then he relented and said, 'We'll have to put them out of their misery, won't we, Marilla? Sorry it's such a public affair, sweetheart, but ... *will* you marry me?'

'I should jolly well think I would,' said Eleanor Marilla St. John brazenly.

Then, suddenly a little shy, they looked at each other uncertainly.

There was a duet from the girls. 'Go on ... kiss her, Uncle Rufus!'

Marilla crumpled into laughter. Rufus caught her by the shoulders, said, smilingly, 'I'll kiss her when she gets her mouth in the right shape for it. Can't be done, laughing.'

She was still shaking with delicious mirth as his lips brushed hers. He turned his head, surveyed two delighted small faces, the faces of the girls. He looked at his nephew and cocked a quizzical eyebrow.

'I've seen much better on TV,' said Anthony Simon

MacGillivray.

Some of the knots wouldn't be unravelled till the children went to bed, but it would have been downright cruel to have banished them there and then.

Suddenly, Tony went across to the set and switched on. Marilla stood entranced, as her father's face came into view. Tony turned a somersault out of sheer high spirits. 'If he only knew what has just happened to his daughter!' he said.

Rufus made a sound and walked straight across to the telephone extension, rang the exchange. He looked over his shoulder before he got an answer, said, 'That programme was live. He'll still be at the studio. I'm going to ask them to put him on to me. I must do the right thing — ask for his daughter's hand.'

Marilla flew across. 'No, Rufus, you'll give the show away to the whole crowd there. Look, I know what it's like to get tangled up in a programme and say too much. You mustn't—'

He said, 'Lay off. I'm only going to speak to your father. Oh, operator, I want the Wellington studios of . . .'

She could only stand there, dumbly, clasping agitated hands.

To say the Reverend Angus St. John got a shock was an understatement. To say he was pleased was another. He began to laugh. 'We had a very evasive phone call from Guy, but my wife read between the lines. She promptly phoned Elfreda in Wanaka and dragged more out of her. Yes, you can have her. I wish you joy of her, getting into a scrape like this. If it hadn't been that you've been so cut off, I'd have been down long since sorting things out. I'll have a word with that erring daughter of mine, then I'll hang up and let you ring her mother. She's at home, so are the twins. It's going to cost you an awful lot of money, young man.'

Rufus laughed. 'It's going to cost a lot more than a call to Wellington, Mr. St. John. I know exactly where my own parents are — they're visiting my sister Kathleen in

London. They got there yesterday. Just imagine how they'll feel when they know their scheme for getting me married paid off.'

Marilla was sparkling-eyed when she was talking to her father. 'You and Mother *must* fly down, Dad. You can come in by chopper. Please try to get the time off.' She laughed, near to tears again. 'It began with a television programme and ended with one. Dad, I must go, and let Rufus get his call through to London,' she turned and surveyed Rufus saucily, 'you see, I want to make quite sure of him. Once he's announced it to the world he can hardly go back on me, even if he has second thoughts. Rufus! Stop it . . . Dad'll hear that!'

The Reverend Angus St. John gave a guffaw that just about shattered Marilla's hearing. 'He did,' he said, and hung up.

Rufus booked the call for eleven o'clock. 'That'll be morning there. My guess is that they won't have gone out. They'd have a long sleep-in after flying from Canada the day before, and will still be talking to Kathy flat out. That gives us time for the other calls. Your mother next.'

Marilla's mother was a relieved woman, and a happy one. She spoke longer to Rufus than to Marilla. Then Rufus said, 'We'll ring Diana. I only wish that I could see her face when I tell her I've just got engaged to the redoubtable Miss Sinjin. Then I'll tell her it's this Marilla St. John, whom, apparently, they saw on television and decided was the wife for me.'

There was a sort of squeak from the three children. Rufus looked at them reflectively. 'What's that meant to mean?' To his amazement they went into a whispering huddle. Then Tony cleared his throat. 'We think we ought to tell you Mum knows.'

Marilla and Rufus boggled at them. Then Rufus said, 'But how could she? And could *you* know *she* knows? You've never as much as spoken to her on the phone. I've been praying she wouldn't. Though it's a wonder she hasn't.'

The girls were in the giggles again. 'But she did ring,'

got out Jane. Anne rushed in, 'One afternoon Marilla had left us because there was an awful fuss going on in the fowl-house. We all wanted to go, but she made us get on with our work, and Mum asked us how we were getting on with Miss Sinjin. Of course, we called her Marilla.'

Tony took it up. 'She just about yelled our heads off, repeating the name. We thought it was only because of Marilla of Green Gables. We thought she'd gone mad when she said she couldn't explain now, but not to let on to that chump of a brother of hers that she now knew Miss Sinjin was Marilla. She actually bribed us, said if we didn't let on she'd bring us each an extra present from up in Auckland. Gee, I was terrified the girls would let it out. Never known them keep a secret before. We couldn't imagine what it was all about, though.'

'I shall probably slit my sister's throat for her when I see her,' said Rufus. 'All right ... I'll ring her just the same, while I'm in a good mood. Wonder what she thought.'

He soon found out. Di was laughing, happy. Donal had been discharged just that day. In two or three days' time they would fly down to Wanaka, to the crib. The whole family could come out by helicopter to see them. She said she had been so mystified, to think this Marilla St. John had arrived at Blue Canyon so speedily, and that Rufus was being so stupid about her, she'd rung Brigid Granville, and got hold of Elfreda. Yes, of course the TV programme had been the only reason they'd thought it ideal. They'd never set eyes on Marilla in the flesh, or had any correspondence with her. It had been only through Brigid they had heard of her. The children all had a say, describing everything with great gusto. Diana promised Tony some fabulous fitment for his telescope, and the two girls new doll's prams each in reward for them having kept her secret. Di added, 'Rufus, you won't have to do too much explaining to Mother and Dad and Kathy ... that'll save you lots of minutes at two dollars each ... I wrote and told them I'd no idea what you were up to, but I thought you'd fallen hard. That was after I'd rung

Elfreda. That letter would be awaiting them.'

The children refused to go to bed till all the phoning was done. While they waited for the phone call to London, they managed to get Elfreda and Stephen, staying with Brigid, and to find out where Guy was staying. Then the London call came through, clear as church bells on the midnight air . . . it was all very heartwarming to Marilla, speaking to in-laws she hadn't met yet, but knew she was going to love. 'You are not to shorten your visit in any way, my dears. Donal and Diana will get home, we'll get access of sorts, and by the time the wedding is on, you'll be back home and maybe the bridge will even be built. I'm sorry you won't be here for Stephen and Elfreda's wedding, because Elfreda said you were lovely to her, long ago, when she was so shy and solitary. But they won't want any more time to get away from them. Here are the children . . . say hullo to Nanny and Granddad and your aunty. Bye-bye for now.'

When the children had been persuaded to put the receiver down, they thought of something else that might delay their bed-time still further. After all, they could probably get away with anything tonight. 'Well, haven't we been mean?' said Jane airily. 'We've told them in London, but Evan and Coll and Buck don't know yet. I'll just go and get them.'

Her uncle swooped. 'No, you don't, poppet. It's bed now. They can be told in the morning. You'll never be able to do your lessons tomorrow. You'll be asleep over your books.'

They all kissed Marilla. Tony looked over his shoulder as they left the room. 'Is that your real reason for shooing us off, Uncle Rufus? I thought you might just have another reason!' He closed the door hurriedly as his uncle picked up a cushion.

Outside, the tree branches stirred and sighed in their sleep, and a young crescent moon gilded the snow on the far peaks. In the kitchen where the big stove incessantly purred, Morag and Magnus's portraits were in shadow. In the garden the thousand flower-buds of the coming summer were lying dormant ... back in the big firelit room, Rufus, having turned the key in the door, crossed to the hearth where Marilla was standing, tall and slender in her white dress, her hair a vivid flame above it.

Rufus's own bright head came nearer. He caught her hands, folded them up against his chest, then slipped his arms about her, drawing her close. The whimsical smile she knew so well lifted the corners of the well-cut mouth ...

'Tony's never seen better than this on television ... that's for sure,' he said, and bent his head.

Have you missed any of these bestselling Harlequin Romances?

Please use the attached order form to indicate your requirements
All titles are available at 75¢ each Offer expires March 31/77.

Please use the attached order form to indicate your requirements
All titles are available at 75¢ each. Offer expires March 31/77.

Harlequin Reader Service
ORDER FORM

MAIL COUPON TO

Harlequin Reader Service,
M.P.O. Box 707,
Niagara Falls, New York 14302.

Canadian SEND Residents TO:

Harlequin Reader Service,
Stratford, Ont. N5A 6W4

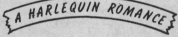
A HARLEQUIN ROMANCE

Please check novels requested

☐ 901	☐ 931	☐ 1025	☐ 1228	☐ 1369	☐ 1400	☐ 1415
☐ 904	☐ 932	☐ 1026	☐ 1230	☐ 1370	☐ 1401	☐ 1417
☐ 905	☐ 967	☐ 1030	☐ 1266	☐ 1373	☐ 1402	☐ 1418
☐ 907	☐ 973	☐ 1036	☐ 1274	☐ 1374	☐ 1403	☐ 1419
☐ 911	☐ 977	☐ 1044	☐ 1354	☐ 1376	☐ 1404	☐ 1421
☐ 913	☐ 985	☐ 1048	☐ 1356	☐ 1377	☐ 1406	☐ 1422
☐ 915	☐ 1004	☐ 1107	☐ 1357	☐ 1378	☐ 1407	☐ 1425
☐ 918	☐ 1005	☐ 1109	☐ 1358	☐ 1379	☐ 1410	☐ 1429
☐ 920	☐ 1006	☐ 1117	☐ 1360	☐ 1381	☐ 1411	☐ 1505
☐ 924	☐ 1011	☐ 1122	☐ 1362	☐ 1386	☐ 1412	
☐ 925	☐ 1013	☐ 1125	☐ 1364	☐ 1387	☐ 1413	
☐ 927	☐ 1019	☐ 1136	☐ 1366	☐ 1389	☐ 1414	

Please send me by return mail the books which I have checked.
I am enclosing 75¢ for each book ordered

Number of books ordered_____ @ 75¢ each = $_____

Postage and Handling =   .25

TOTAL = $_____

Name_____

Address_____

City_____

State/Prov._____

Zip/Postal Code_____

Harlequin Presents...

BY POPULAR DEMAND . . .

36 original novels from this series — by 3 of the world's greatest romance authors.

These back issues by Anne Hampson, Anne Mather, and Violet Winspear have been out of print for some time. So don't miss out, order your copies now!

All the above titles are available at 95¢ each. Please use the attached order form to indicate your requirements.
Offer expires March 31, 1977.

Harlequin Reader Service

ORDER FORM

MAIL COUPON TO → Harlequin Reader Service,
M.P.O. Box 707,
Niagara Falls. New York 14302.

Canadian SEND Residents TO: → Harlequin Reader Service,
Stratford, Ont. N5A 6W4

Harlequin Presents...

Please check Volumes requested:

☐ 1	☐ 2	☐ 3	☐ 4	☐ 5
☐ 7	☐ 8	☐ 9	☐ 10	☐ 11
☐ 12	☐ 13	☐ 14	☐ 15	☐ 16
☐ 17	☐ 18	☐ 19	☐ 20	☐ 21
☐ 22	☐ 23	☐ 24	☐ 25	☐ 26
☐ 27	☐ 28	☐ 29	☐ 30	☐ 31
☐ 32	☐ 33	☐ 34	☐ 35	☐ 36
☐ 37				

Please send me by return mail the books which I have checked.
I am enclosing 95¢ for each book ordered

Number of books ordered _____ @ 95¢ each = $ _____

Postage and Handling = .25

TOTAL = $ _____

Name _____

Address _____

City _____

State/Prov. _____

Zip/Postal Code _____